I0537096

Ferd scowled and, looking directly into Bat Hardin's face, said, "I can't become your deputy. I'm a paroled convict."

"That doesn't matter to me," Bat answered quickly. "This is an emergency. I need you."

"You don't understand, Bat. I *can't* help you, no matter what the reason. You see, I have a bug planted in my skull."

"A what?"

"An electronic bug. The Meritocracy has made some recent changes in penology that most people don't know about. Most convicted criminals—even lifers, like me—aren't kept in prison. We carry these implanted bugs that monitor every word we say, all our actions. I can carry on a reasonably normal life, but the government has a continual fix on me. If I do or say anything that's restricted, I get these terrible headaches—they can even kill me."

Bat said, uncomfortably, "What . . . well, what were you sentenced for?"

"Conspiracy to commit subversive acts against the Meritocracy. . . ."

ROLLTOWN

by
MACK REYNOLDS

WILDSIDE PRESS

ROLLTOWN

Copyright ©, 1976 by Mack Reynolds

A shorter version of this novel was published in *Galaxy Magazine* under the title THE TOWNS MUST ROLL

Also by Mack Reynolds

ABILITY QUOTIENT
BLACKMAN'S BURDEN
BORDER, BREED NOR BIRTH
COMPUTER WAR
CODE DUELLO
DAY AFTER TOMORROW
DEPRESSION OR BUST
DAWNMAN PLANET
LOOKING BACKWARD FROM THE YEAR 2000
PLANETARY AGENT X
THE RIVAL RIGELLIANS
SATELLITE CITY
SECTION G: UNITED PLANETS
SPACE BARBARIANS
TOMORROW MIGHT BE DIFFERENT

I

Bat Hardin was getting fully immersed in his book when Ferd Zogbaum's knock came on the door. He gave a grunt of displeasure, marked his page and got up.

Ferd's camper was on the slow and awkward side, comparatively, so Bat suggested that they take his electro-steamer. Linares proper was about a kilometer down the road and it took them only minutes to arrive.

On the way, Bat said, "What do you expect to find?"

"Darned if I know," Ferd said grumpily. "It wasn't my idea to go into town. It was yours."

Bat said, "I thought we'd just scout around a little. Do you speak Spanish?"

"No. A little German."

"That'll do us a hell of a lot of good," Bat said. "A great couple of snoopers we'll be. About all I can say in Spanish is *una mas cerveza, por favor.*"

"What does that mean?"

"Another beer, please."

"Great," Ferd grinned sourly. "We'd better make a beeline for a bar, then."

The town of Linares boasted a population of approximately 14,000 and had little call to fame. The area was not particularly suited to farming, mining nor, certainly, industry, and since its scenic attractions were only fair, tourism was also a matter of little gain. Thus it was that the community had hardly participated in the growth of

1

Mexico proper such as the progressive cities of Monterrey, Guadalajara, Vera Cruz and above all Mexico City itself. In fact, Linares remained a town of yesteryear, a sleepy, dull and, at this time of the year, at least, dusty backwash to the days of Pancho Villa.

The main highway leading west and, further on, south, compounded insult to injury by avoiding Linares proper. Bat and Ferd had to take a side street to the village zocco or plaza, the center about which every Mexican hamlet, village or city revolves.

It differed not at all, except possibly being amongst the least picturesque in all the Republic, from the norm. There was a park, a bandstand in its center, iron benches about the perimeter, patches of sad flowers spotted here and there. A score of trees provided perching for multitudes of birds which evidently had no respect for weary townsmen slumped below on the benches.

There were few cars parked about the square, and those that were there were more often old-fashioned internal combustion engines, rather than steamers or the more recent electro-steamers. Evidently, pollution laws had never been enforced in Mexico. In fact, of wheeled vehicles there were more beaten up trucks and buses than private cars.

"A cantina it is," Bat muttered. "I wonder if anybody else from New Woodstock has come in."

"I doubt it," Ferd said. "Everybody's tired. Maybe tomorrow, somebody'll get up the gumption. Most of the community's never been in Mexico before. There's one over there. Dig that. I don't believe I've ever seen swinging doors on a bar outside a historic TV show before."

Bat Hardin parked the electro-steamer in front of the bar in question and got out, Ferd doing the same on the other side.

2

Three or four indolent villagers, leaning up against adobe wall or lamppost, seemed to take displeasure when Bat locked the car doors. He wondered idly if it was because they were thwarted in going through the vehicle, or if they were objecting to his suggesting that it might be done if he failed to lock up. Come to think of it, Bat recalled that in these small towns, at least, the crime rate was said to be infinitesimal, though it could be different in the larger, more sophisticated cities. What crime there was usually consisted of violence between family members or between different families, usually involving passion or feud, rather than pilferage or robbery committed against foreigners. However, he still locked the car.

Ferd led the way through the swinging doors. If the town as a whole had reminded them of a movie set based on the Mexican revolution of 1910, there was little in the interior that would indicate the bar wasn't a continuation of the set. The room was long, the walls decorated with bullfight posters and illustrations of bountifully bosomed Playmates, probably long deceased, along with the magazine which had once built its reputation with them. There was a brass rail along the bottom of the bar and a tile trough with running water for those who must needs expectorate. At the far end of the bar, along the whole wall which faced the door was a tile urinal which could easily have accommodated half a dozen beer-drinking customers at a time. There was a stench of stale urine in the air, along with that of unwashed bodies. Obviously this was a resort that did not cater to women, not to speak of catering to ladies.

There were perhaps twenty imbibers present, leaning on a prehistoric bar that would have accommodated double the number. Behind it were three bartenders; one, a fifty-year-old pushing three hundred pounds in weight, was

3

obviously the proprietor, the others, two youngsters in their teens. The liquor selection was limited; tequila, mescal, rum and gin. A battered refrigerator indicated that at least the beer and coke would be cold.

Ferd muttered from the side of his mouth, even as they found a place, "Montezuma drank here."

"Or at least, Cortes," Bat muttered back. "I've recently become an authority on the subject. According to the books, the Aztecs didn't drink anything but pulque."

A silence had fallen upon their entry. The two Americans ignored it.

The proprietor, who puffed slightly upon movement, hesitated for a long moment but finally came down to them, ignoring some of the cold stares of his regular customers.

He stood before them, both obscenely fat hands on the bar and said, expressionlessly, "Senors?"

Bat said to Ferd, "First day in Mexico. Nothing would do except tequila."

"Right as rain."

"Tequila, por favor," Bat said to the bartender.

The other nodded, turned and secured a bottle of the white liquid nuclear bomb, a saucer of limes cut into quarters and a shaker of salt.

He muttered, barely audibly, "Salud," and turned away.

"Jesus," Ferd said. "The hospitality around here is boundless."

Both Bat and Ferd had been in the country before and knew the routine. They poured themselves drinks that would have been called triples in the States into the shot glasses, took up the salt in turn and sprinkled a touch of it on the back of their left hands. They touched their tongues to the salt, tossed the tequila back in one fell

4

swoop, then grabbed up a quarter of the lime and bit into it.

"Wow!" Ferd said, half in appreciation, half in objection to the strength of the fiery product of the maguey plant.

The Mexican, standing nearest to them at Bat's left, sneered and said in passable English, "Ah, not enough macho for tequila, eh, gringo?"

Ferd hesitated for a moment. Finally, he said to Bat, "Well, we came here to learn. What does macho mean?"

Bat said quietly, "Manliness, more or less. The quality of being a real man." He was nibbling unhappily at his lower lip.

"And gringo?"

"It's a derogatory word for an American. Why it should be derogatory, I wouldn't know. Evidently, it comes down from the Mexican War days. When the American troops invaded from Texas and Vera Cruz one of the popular songs of the day was Robert Burns' "Green Grow the Rushes, Oh" and the Americans sang it as a marching tune. The Mexicans of the time took the first two words and called the unwelcome invaders 'green grows', or 'gringos'. It bears a sneering connotation."

"Thanks for the lecture," Ferd said politely. He turned to the Mexican. "And you're a greaser."

"Holy *Smokes* . . ." Bat began in protest, and much too late.

The Mexican, although a small man by the standards of either of the two foreigners, with a sweep of his right arm pushed Bat Harden to the side that he all but fell onto the wall behind them.

The Mexican moved in fast, so fast that he should have been upon Ferd before that worthy could erect defenses.

5

However, the American was prepared. Ferd went backward in the one, two, three shuffle of the trained pugilist, his hands coming up in fists.

The Mexican was ardent but fighting out of his class as well as weight, height and reach. He swung once, twice, wildly. And then Ferd Zogbaum stepped in with a classic feint of the left and then a crushing blow into the other's stomach with his right.

Bat Hardin, meanwhile, had found his feet again and turned to meet the rush of the other occupants of the bar. Unlike his companion, he adopted a crouching stance, his hands slightly forward and held as choppers, rather than fists. He had not spent his long years in the Asian War without compiling background in hand-to-hand combat.

The very number of the others, in the confined space of the cantina, was their handicap. That and the fact that the locals had been doing a considerable amount of drinking before the arrival of the strangers. They had the spirit of the thing completely, but precious little science. While his companion was finishing off his attacker, Bat was able to hold them although he was being pushed back by sheer weight.

Ferd yelled, "Let's get out of here, Bat!"

But Bat was nearly eliminated from the fray at this point by an attack on his flank. The bartender, with something that looked like a child's baseball bat in one of his fat paws, leaned over the bar and with surprising speed took a massive swing at the embattled American. Bat caught the motion from the side of his eye and tried to swing away from the blow but only partially succeeded and for a moment the fog seemed to roll in when the bludgeon struck him glancingly on the side of his head.

6

Ferd caught him, supported him just long enough for the other to shake his head in an attempt to clear it.

Swinging almost as wildly as the charging locals now, the two shuffled backward toward the swinging doors.

"I'll try to hold them," Ferd yelled. "Get the car door open!"

It was the obvious strategy. Bat turned quickly and made a dash for it. In the street, he straight-armed one of the loungers who had been outside and who was now coming up on the run, obviously attracted by the sounds of the battle. Another was coming from the opposite direction, a smallish youngster probably not out of his teens. However, Bat Hardin had neither time nor patience for compassion. He slugged the younger man in the face, putting him down, and tore his car keys from his pocket. He fumbled at the door's lock, and felt arms grasping him from the rear. He reached back, snagged an arm and threw the other brutally over his shoulder in the old wrestler's favorite hold, the Flying Mare.

Ferd Zogbaum erupted from the cantina and slammed the doors back into the faces of the enraged enemy.

The car door was open. Bat Hardin darted in and snaked across the seat to the driver's position. Ferd was still holding the rapidly emerging local citizens, his arms swinging like windmills. Bat reached out and grabbed him by the belt and pulled him bodily inside in a sprawl.

The car began to move forward. Bat deliberately held down his speed so as not to seriously harm the two or three of the enemy who were immediately ahead, trying to stop him. They scurried to either side as he slowly speeded up. A few were already heaving rocks, which bounded off the car's side.

7

Ferd had finally managed to sit erect and now slammed shut the still open door on his side. "Fun and games!" he yelped. "Get us the hell out of here, Bat. If any of those jokers are heeled, we've had it."

Bat growled, "This is a converted police riot car. They'd have to have anti-tank guns."

They were back on the main road leading out of town and to the site where New Woodstock was parked.

"Armored, eh?" Ferd said and then, "Hey, you've got a nasty cut on your head." He pulled forth a handkerchief and handed it over. "This is clean." Then he put a hand to his own head and groaned.

Bat Hardin, driving with one hand, held the handkerchief to the cut. "What the hell's the matter?" he said. "If there'd been any gunfire, I'd say you'd copped one."

"Splitting headache," Ferd muttered. "I always get them, if I get into a fight."

"By Christ," Bat said bitterly. "I always thought of you as an easygoing character. What the hell was the idea of calling that guy a greaser? Haven't you ever heard that a gentle answer turneth away rats?"

"Yeah, and you can lead a horse to water but you can't make her," Ferd groaned, still holding his head. "Listen, we had no more chance of getting out of that joint without a scrap than we have of flying without wings. Couldn't you feel that in the air when we walked in? That bartender would have slipped us a mickey, if he'd had one handy. I just precipitated it before they got organized—thank God."

"More of your feminine intuition?" Bat said in disgust. He dabbed at his head and looked at the handkerchief. He was bleeding profusely. "I'll have to take this to Doc," he growled.

They were approaching the camp site.

8

Ferd looked over his shoulder. "None of them coming —yet."

"They won't come," Bat said, still in disgust. "There weren't more than twenty or so of them, most of them tight. If we stuck around here for any length of time at all, they might stir up enough of the other townspeople to help them give us a hard time, but as of right now they'd be outnumbered. I suspect that the local cops, at this moment, are cooling them."

He pulled up before the mobile town's clinic.

Doc Barnes was sitting in a folding chair out front talking to his nurse who was also relaxed in the cool of the evening.

Ferd muttered, "This head is killing me. I'll go over to my own place. See you later, Bat." He stumbled from the vehicle, head still in hands, and staggered away.

II

New Woodstock had crossed the Rio Grande at Mc-Allen and passed through the Mexican city of Reynosa.

There had been two fairly major sites on the American side of the border with excellent facilities for as many as ten thousand homes apiece but Bat Hardin and the executive committee had checked to find that the next nearest site was at Linares, a full 254 kilometers to the southwest. They wanted to push on through and avoid the necessity of setting up for the night at some second class or emergency site where there would be inadequate supply facilities and other shortcomings. There would be enough of that when they got down into Central America and beyond.

The committee had handled all the required border formalities the day before so that there was nothing to hold them up. Bat Hardin leading, as usual, they strung out along the highway, some fiive hundred homes strong, with the auxiliary vehicles spaced periodically between them. Most of the homes were drawn by fairly modern electro-steamers but when you were dealing with even five hundred mobile homes you could hardly expect very often to get through one whole day without some needed minor repairs.

The stretch from Reynosa to the little town of China, where they branched off onto a side road so as to avoid the large city of Monterrey, was excellent enough. Above ground, of course, and not automated as would have

10

been an American road of this size, but adequate. Even the Pan American Highway was far from completely automated and this was not the Pan American Highway as yet. They'd join that further south.

Bat rode alone in his converted police vehicle, drawing his moderately-sized mobile home behind. He was far from a misogynist but at this junction in his life he had no permanent feminine affiliations and, for some reason not quite clear to even himself, he desired none. He was a fairly tall man with a military carriage and a habitually worried expression. His hair was crisp, his complexion dark and his features so heavy that he would hardly have been thought of as handsome by average American standards. He had a nervous habit of gnawing on his underlip at the slightest of problems.

He wore a khaki semi-uniform. Local police often had a chip on their shoulders in their attitude toward the pseudo-police of the mobile towns, who, after all, had no authority in the areas through which they passed. Law in the mobile towns was largely a voluntary matter—minor infractions could be taken care of in the community but on any major matter it was necessary to call in the proper authorities of whatever area the town was in at the time. Yes, it was all very voluntary; however, there was a certain moral obligation to abide by the decisions of the easygoing town officials and that member of the community who persisted in revolt against community rules was soon invited to take himself off. It was the ultimate punishment that could be inflicted and for all practical purposes the only one save ostracism.

This part of Mexico was not particularly attractive as areas Bat had known from earlier trips but the site at which they were to stay that evening was at the edge of the mountains and on the banks of a stream. And the following day they should be getting into the Mexico famed in story and song.

At the thought of that Bat Hardin grunted deprecation. The world was becoming one in more than one sense. The larger cities, in particular, such as still existed at least, were becoming unbelievably alike. Somehow or other, they all seemed to look like Cincinnati. He was hoping that it would be different in South America. It was said that many areas of South America still resisted what was sometimes called the Coca-Colaization of the world.

A mobile town, like a convoy of ships in wartime, moves at the speed of its slowest member. Alone, Bat Hardin's electro-steamer could easily maintain a steady five hundred kilometers an hour, at least on an automated underground ultra-highway in the States. Even under manual control such as at present, three hundred kilometers an hour was quite possible. However, the average home behind him seldom got much above a hundred kilometers an hour, especially when traveling in a group.

He shrugged that off. He was used to this reduced speed and they were in no hurry. No hurry at all. If they wished, they could take a year—or ten years—to reach their destination. He grunted at that, too. In actuality, they were rather vague on just what the destination was.

What was really on his mind was the sullen quality that he had seemed to detect in some of the border officials. It was nothing he could quite put his finger upon and didn't apply to all of the immigrations and customs people, but it was there in most. And he didn't quite know why.

He said into his car phone, "New Woodstock, Al Castro."

Al's face faded in. "The rear guard here," he said, yawning. "I'll sure as hell be glad when we get up into the mountains. I hate air conditioning."

Bat ignored the complaint of his second. Al Castro was a born complainer. He would have complained about Peter's gate service, and the tone of Gabriel's horn.

He was a small man of about thirty-fiive. Thin and wiry, and absolutely reliable in the clutch. He was Bat's right hand man, and the town cop would have hated to see the other leave New Woodstock.

Bat said, "Anybody fallen behind so far?"

Al Castro shook his head. "Surprise, surprise, no. Of course, we got well-organized before crossing the border. So we all got off together. But two will get you ten that by the time the lead homes get to Mexico City, we'll be strung out over several hundred kilometers."

"Don't I know it? No bet," Bat groaned. "I suppose what we'll have to do is rendezvous there, stay several days sightseeing and waiting for the stragglers to catch up."

"Yeah, I suppose so. We'll be ready for a rest by then anyway."

"I'll take it up with the executive committee," Bat said. "Let me know if anybody drops out before we reach Linares. See you, Al." He deactivated the phone.

They were only to spend the one night in the Linares camp site so they made no particular efforts to arrange themselves in predetermined order; except, of course, that the administration and other auxiliary vehicles were parked in the center of their group. They occupied only about a third of the site's most favored area, and aside from their own town there were only half a dozen other mobile homes. The site was large by New Woodstock's needs but Bat Hardin wondered what would happen if a really large town came through. However, he supposed a really large mobile town wouldn't come through the by-ways such as this. They stuck to the Pan American Highway and came down through Laredo, Monterrey and Saltillo.

Bat himself parked near the administration building, noting that the driver, Milt Waterman, wasn't bothering to set it up but was making his way over to his father's home to rejoin his family. Milt usually drove the heavy steamer that drew the administration building but not always. There were other volunteers. In fact, of all the auxiliaries the ad building seemed to have some sort of mystic prestige. Bat supposed that Dean Armanruder had informed the youngster that for this short a stay, there would be no need for the offices.

Bat detached his electro-steamer from his home, to have it ready in case of emergency, but left it to wander about on foot on the off chance that he could be of some assistance to someone setting up one of the larger and consequently more awkward homes. Jim Blake, for instance, could usually use an extra hand. Jim might be one of the most prominent artists in New Woodstock but he wasn't mechanically-minded enough to wind a clock.

Blake, however, had secured the services of one of his neighbors who didn't have to set up since his home was a single unit. Ferd Zogbaum, a bachelor, lived in what was usually called a camper, a very compact bus-like vehicle that combined the electro-steamer and living quarters very neatly. Ferd was usually on hand to help out when help was called for. A damn good member of the community, Bat had long since decided.

Clarke and Benton as usual were having a squabble over who parked where. For some reason, known only

14

to themselves, they invariably parked side by side and invariably got into a spat. Bat was of the opinion that they were in actuality as good friends as were their wives but that neither would admit it. He stopped long enough to put in a mild word of suggestion and they grudgingly abided by it.

Everything seemed to be settled down and Bat Hardin fell in beside Dag Stryn, the guru of the New Temple, and elderly Doc Barnes, leading toward the site's ultramarket.

He said to the town's doctor, "How's Mrs. Terwilliger?"

Doc Barnes said, "She'll be all right, Bat. I haven't the facilities in the clinic to handle her operation but I'll stop off with her at the first city with an adequate hospital. I have her in stasis for the time being."

"She and Phil will have to drop behind?" Bat said, nibbling his lower lip.

"Not necessarily. She can convalesce in the clinic while we're underway."

Dag Stryn, a blond Viking of a man but almost unbelievably gentle in all things, said, "I'm worried about the Terwilligers. They're our oldest and I'm just wondering if this protracted a trip is the sort of thing they should be doing."

"Basically they're both as strong as horses," Barnes told him. "They'll be all right. You can't just sit and die because you've reached your seventies."

The doctor must know, Bat thought. He was certainly pushing that age himself.

They reached the ultra-market and stood at the end of a short line that had formed.

When his turn came, Bat took up a number key and walked on past the display shelves, periodically stopping

15

before an item he wished and touching his key to the impulse device. Largely, the items in stock were familiar and again he thought about how the world was becoming one. Aside from a few items such as tortillas and an inordinate selection of chili peppers, he could have been in an ultra-market in Maine or Oregon. Today, seemingly, the Australians ate the same food, wore the same clothes, lived in the same type house and enjoyed the same entertainment as did a South African, an Argentine, or an Alaskan Eskimo.

He wasn't, he realized, particularly happy about the fact. It must have been interesting, in the old days, to be able to witness different cultures, eat exotic foods, sample different drinks, ogle girls attired in saris or sarongs, rather than the now practically universal Western world fashions.

His selections all made, he returned to the delivery counter, put his number key in place and then slipped his pocket phone cum credit card in the appropriate slot. Within moments, his package erupted from the delivery chute and he picked it up and headed for the door.

In turning abruptly, he caromed against one of the new community members named Jeff Smith.

"Hey, watch yourself, boy," the other snapped.

"Sorry," Bat said mildly.

Smith grumbled something inarticulately and made off.

Bat looked after him for a moment. Jeff Smith was a feisty little man of about thirty-five, fairly recent to New Woodstock and thus far hadn't picked up much in the way of close companions. He was supposedly a composer and had a small piano in his unusually large mobile home. Bat occasionally heard rambling music from the Smith quarters but to this point the other had never offered to play any of his compositions or anything else at the community entertainments. For that matter, he seldom attended these though he, like Bat, was one of the unattached men in New Woodstock.

Bat shrugged and continued on his way. He hoped that Jeff Smith worked out. In a mobile town there was small room for soreheads. You were either a tight community of cooperating fellows or you soon came apart as a town and dispersed to seek better companionship elsewhere. Bat Hardin liked New Woodstock and would have hated to see anything happen to it. It was unique as mobile towns went; in fact, to his knowledge, there simply weren't any other mobile art colonies, at least not in North America.

III

He left his purchases in his home, decided to postpone his evening meal and walked around the site a bit more. In actuality, he was hoping to get an invitation to share a meal with one of the families which boasted a better cook than Bat would ever become. Preparing food for a single individual isn't conducive to haute cuisine and Bat usually wound up heating a prepared dinner, a form of stoking the furnace of which he was contemptuous. He pondered the desirability of teaming together with some of the other singles, such as Diana Sward, Ferd Zogbaum and, were the other a bit more compatible, possibly Jeff Smith, and taking turns cooking; not that he knew whether or not the others were any better in a mini-kitchen then he was.

Speaking of Diana Sward, he came upon the girl sitting in a folding chair before her mobile home, an easel before her, a palette in hand and a scowl on her face. She was obviously trying to get the colorful mountain peaks to the west on her canvas.

Bat said, "Hi, Di."

She muttered, "The damn light is off. This Mexican light is different. You'd think it would be the same as similar countryside up in California, or wherever, but it isn't."

Bat said mildly, "How can light be different? Light is light."

18

"That shows how much you know about it," she snorted. "Sit down, Bat."

He looked about him for a seat, found none, then went over to her trailer, opened the front door, stepped into the impossibly cluttered interior, threw some things off of a chair and onto the couch, and took the chair outside, setting it up across from her.

She was potentially a very pretty young woman but made small effort to realize her potentialities. On the few occasions when she bothered to do herself up for some community affair or whatever, she wowed them all, looking surprisingly like a brunette version of the onetime movie star Marilyn Monroe, though it was unlikely that any of the residents of New Woodstock would have remembered that far back.

Now she was attired in nothing save a pair of somewhat paint bespattered shorts and a streak of blue down her right cheek where she had obviously touched her brush in an absentminded moment of irritation. She was topless, and it was Bat's opinion that she had the most magnificent pair of mammary glands he had ever seen.

She said, "The hell with it," and tossed the brush to the shelf of the easel. "I wonder if I'm going to get this all the way down to South America. I shoulda stood in Colorado." She relaxed back into her chair and stifled a yawn.

"What's up?" she said.

"Not much," Bat answered. He looked at the hardly begun oil painting.

"Are you any good, Di?" he said in a friendly dig.

She grunted her disgust and scratched her bare stomach unconsciously as she thought about it. "Not very, but I make a modest living. I have a show or two a year

19

and that usually puts me over the hump. Three or four idiots collect my stuff."

He was moderately surprised. "You mean you don't have to live on NIT?"

"NIT is for nitwits," she retorted. "Besides, I'm not eligible for it."

"How do you mean? I thought three-quarters of this whole town depended on NIT. Surely I do."

"I'm an alien."

"We're all aliens in Mexico."

"I mean, I'm an alien in the United States. I'm not eligible for the Negative Income Tax." Then she added, inconsistently, in view of her crack about nitwits, "Damn it."

"I didn't know that," Bat said. "You talk like an American."

"I came over from Common Europe as a youngster. When the Germanies reunited, my mother had to hustle out. Some of the new authorities weren't too happy about the stand she had taken in the old days. My name's actually Diana von Sward und Hanse. Very impressive, eh? She was a Grafin."

"A what?"

"Something like a countess from way back in the Kaiser's day. She was also on the chauvinistic side and didn't want to become an American. Since she seemingly had all the money she, and I, would need, she didn't become a citizen. By the time she lost her capital—mother was an ass with money—it wasn't as easy as all that to become an American. With the advent of NIT practically everybody in the world would have become a citizen if the government would have allowed it."

She changed the subject. "Bat, what in the hell are you doing in New Woodstock?"

He shrugged. "Why not?"

"You're not really interested in any of the arts."

"I'm interested in all of them."

"I meant, you don't participate in any of them."

He shrugged again. He liked this lusty girl, liked her company. "In any mobile town, even an art colony, you need other than artists, writers, musicians, sculptors, and the rest. You need, for instance, a cop or two."

"Sure, but I mean, what do you get out of it? There's no pay goes with your position. It's voluntary. Like you said, you live on NIT."

Bat thought about it, or at least pretended to. He already knew the answer.

He said slowly, "I'm not a loafer by nature. Besides, I feel a need to identify, I suppose you'd call it. Be part of the community." He added, "I want to do my share——"

"You do more than your share," she said in an unwontedly soft voice.

". . .carry my part of the load," he finished. He thought some more. "I'm a cop, for free. Some of the others who don't spend full time at their art act in helping on repairs, as car mechanics, electricians, tinkerers, teachers or whatever. For instance, why do you teach art classes to the kids three times a week?"

"Touché," she snorted. "But what I meant was, if you're ambitious to work, don't want to be a loafer as you called it, why do you stay in a community like this? Why the hell not get yourself a job up in the States?"

"Hiiii," he sighed. "Haven't you heard of the Meritocracy?"

21

"Come again?"

"Di, old girl, we have a new socio-economic system in our America. Symbols die hard, labels die hard, but today such labels as democracy, capitalism, free enterprise and such are passé. We have Meritocracy. It's a term that came in back in the 1950s or 1960s I think and it was starting even then."

"All right," she told him. "Drop the other shoe. So what's Meritocracy?"

"Well, back when the United States was first formed, about 80 percent of the population was involved in agriculture, most of the rest in the other primary occupations such as fishing, forestry, hunting and mining. At that point, only a few were in secondary occupations concerned with processing the products of a primary occupation. Practically none were in tertiary occupations which render services to primary and secondary fields. Came the industrial revolution, however, and the secondary occupations overtook the primary and by the middle of the 20th century or so only five percent of the population was needed in agriculture and tertiary workers were growing rapidly in number. With the second industrial revolution, call it automation or the computer economy if you will, even the secondary occupations began to fall off. The blue collar worker gave way to the white collar employee. Even on the farm the technician took the place of the illiterate behind the plow, the mechanical cotton pickers the place of the darky plodding down the endless cotton rows dragging his sack.

"But still that wasn't the end. The quaternary occupations began to take precedence; occupations that render services to tertiary occupations or to each other. They are heavily concentrated among agencies of government, the professions, the arts, the nonprofit groups and the like. And along in here came the Meritocracy with the amalgamation of practically all information possessed by the human race into the National Data Banks of the computerized world."

He took a deep breath. "Because, Di, old girl, in those data banks is *all* the information obtainable about all of our people; all the dope that used to be involved in the census reports, the tax records, the Social Security records, your educational standing, your military record, your medical records, your employment records and so forth and so on, but above all your I.Q."

Di said, scowling at his bitter tone, "I seem to have missed a curve there."

"No. At the same time Meritocracy took over, the full impact of automation hit us. It hadn't been so bad when it struck the primary occupations, although one devil of a lot of the rural population were forced into the cities to try and find work, or, if not, relief. But by this time both the secondary and primary occupations were on the skids, numerically speaking. Five percent of our population could operate our farms and farm them more profitably than they had ever been farmed before. A fraction of the working force would operate the mines and mills, the factories and other industries. But when the automation hit the tertiary occupations, then, of a sudden, the majority of the population became occupationally displaced. It had come to the point where sales and services were employing the majority. Overnight, comparatively, that changed. The old system of bringing the product to the consumer was antiquated as was no other branch of our socio-economic system. Hundreds of thousands of individually operated stores, dispensing

23

the same products, had been the past. Hundreds of thousands of repairmen, servicemen, tinkerers, had been involved in keeping our gadgets in repair.

"Very well. The ultra-market finished off the small shopkeepers in much the same manner that agricultural automation finished off the small farmer. And automation also finished off the small repairman when it became cheaper to throw away a mixer, a refrigeration power unit, or even a TV set or the replaceable engine of a car than it was to repair it."

Di said in impatience, "What's all this got to do with your Meritocracy?"

"Just this. The majority of our population became unneeded in our socio-economic system. What John Kenneth Galbraith, the old economist, once called the Technostructure, in short, management, became for all practical purposes all of the working population. Practically everybody who worked was part of management; from scientists, through engineers to technicians. The blue collar worker was an anachronism. Happily—I guess—by this time production was at such a scale that the unneeded were not forced into starvation. Simultaneously with the advent of Meritocracy came the movement toward Guaranteed Annual Income, the Negative Income Tax and other floors beneath the income of every family in the country, employed usefully or not. In short, the dole."

Diana Sward said, "Goddammit to hell, stop lecturing me largely about things I already know. What's this got to do with you not being a loafer, not going up and getting yourself a job?"

He said bitterly, "There's not enough work to go around, Di. And that which is available requires both I.Q. and education. You need both. I.Q. without education is, of course, worthless, but you need the I.Q. to get the education, in the schools that count, at least. I've never seen figures but I suspect that the average person who works today in American industry has an I.Q. of something like 130. The number that have an I.Q. of a hundred or less must be infinitesimal.

"Di, when you apply for a position with any corporation in the nation, the first thing they do is check your dossier in the National Data Banks. And shortly after your name and identity number is your good old Intelligence Quotient, which they have been testing periodically ever since you entered kindergarten. Di, half the population of the United States is below average, that is, half have I.Q.s of less than 100. When a fraction of the population can hold down all the jobs needed, why should any corporation in its right mind hire somebody with an I.Q. of less than 100?"

"What in the name of Good Jesus has that got to do with you?"

"I've got an I.Q. of 93, Di."

IV

She stared at him. "Don't be ridiculous. Why, you've been lecturing me like a professor of economics for the past twenty minutes."

He made a face. "Don't confuse learning with intelligence, Di. I didn't have much formal schooling. In fact, practically none at all. When I was a kid we still had the ghettos and slums and my family was as lower class as you could get. But during the Asian War I copped one and was in the hospital for quite a spell. I learned to read there. No, I mean literally. Before that I couldn't do much more than read comic books and sign my own name. But I learned to read. You know the first book I read? The Bible, of all things. It made an agnostic out of me but it also goosed my intellectual curiosity." He twisted his worried face into self-deprecation again. "Such as I'm capable of."

"Oh, for crissakes stop drooling self-pity."

"Sorry. At any rate I became a reader. A compulsive reader, an inveterate reader, I suppose you call it. I spend all my free time reading."

"Well, that shows you're really intelligent."

"No it doesn't," he said doggedly. "All it shows is that I'm a compulsive reader. You can be slowish as far as intelligence is concerned and still do a lot of reading. Maybe you don't read as fast as the quiz kid type does, but you wade through it eventually. You even learn the twenty-dollar words, but you mustn't kid yourself, it

26

doesn't make you any smarter. If your I.Q. is 90, it's still 90. And in the Meritocracy it's exposed. There is no room for the stupid."

She tightened her mouth in rejection. "How do you know your I.Q. is 93?"

He chuckled wryly. "When I first entered the army I worked for a while in records. I snuck a look at my examinations. By the way, what's yours?"

She made a gesture of shivering. "I've never tried to find out."

"Any citizen, any alien for that matter, is entitled to check his National Data Bank dossier if he wants to. Gives you a chance to refute any misinformation that might have crept in."

It was her turn to be rueful. "Sure, but I've always been afraid to check up on my I.Q. Afraid that I might be, uh, inadequate."

"I don't blame you," he laughed. "It's the reaction of a good many of us, and probably well-founded. Sometimes, I'm sorry that curiosity ever hit me in the army. I'd be happier if I didn't know."

She leaned forward. "But look, Bat, there are fields in which I.Q. doesn't particularly enter. The arts, for instance. Some of the great artists of the world were lamebrains—excuse me, I shouldn't have used that term."

He spread his hands in a gesture of submission. "Yeah, but I haven't any particular aptitude for any of the arts. Believe me, I've messed around in them."

"But there are other fields——"

"Sure, and I've held down jobs in some. Somebody like I can still be a servant. I used to curry horses for one of the big mucky-mucks in Kentucky. But I don't like being a servant."

"It's honorable work."

27

"All right, but I don't like it."

"In a way, you're a servant now, a public servant."

"All right, once again. But now, here in New Woodstock I'm an honored member of the community. With a few exceptions, I'm welcome in everybody's home. I get invited to the parties; I'm often brought in for lunch or dinner. Hell, the Robertsons named their new baby after me."

She stared at him in frustration.

He said doggedly, "Here I belong. Here I am wanted. Here I can be of use. The Meritocracy doesn't need me and I refuse to sit around in the New America collecting my NIT and not being able to return anything of value to society. I don't like charity. I think it's bad for those who have to take it. Most certainly it is for healthy young people still in their prime."

Jeff Smith, who seemed to be listing slightly to starboard, passed by them, heading back to his home from the direction of the site's cantina.

He glowered at them, his eyes particularly going over Diana Sward's bared bosom. There was an element of sneer in his voice when he slurred, "Yawl having a good time?"

He was past before either of them could think of anything to say.

Bat chuckled and said to her, "I think Jeff sports the last of the southern accents. How does he maintain it in this day of TV and movies? And what's that chip on his shoulder, anyway?"

"He invited me to have a drink a little earlier," Di said distastefully. "I turned him down. He's been trying to lay me ever since I entered the community. Frankly, small men have never appealed to me."

Ferd Zogbaum came up, a scowl on his face. A scowl

wasn't normal on Ferd. He was an easygoing, generous type, pushing thirty, pushing six feet, pushing a hundred and sixty pounds and was as nearly universally liked by everybody in New Woodstock as is possible to be liked without being completely wishy-washy. And Ferd wasn't wishy-washy.

He said, "Hi, folks."

They exchanged the amenities and Di suggested he get himself a chair. She stood. "I think I'd better put on some more clothes, it's cooling off."

Ferd said to Bat, "Could I talk to you a minute?" His tone indicated that he meant alone.

"Sure, why not?" Bat said, coming to his feet. "Let's go over to my place. See you later, Di."

"Right on." Di looked at Ferd. "Don't forget. You were coming over for supper."

He grinned his shy, overgrown-boy grin. "Do I look crazy? You're the best cook in town."

"Flattery will get you nowheres, laddy buck. Besides, at best you could say I'm the nearest thing to a cook in town. Cooking is an art, a lost art, and doesn't even exist any more in an art colony."

Bat and Ferd started to the former's mobile home, sauntering along easily. It was the time of day Bat liked best in the mobile art colony. Two of the younger set, known to be considering marriage, went by slowly, hand in hand. The boy had a blanket over one arm. They were probably strolling down to the river bank for a quick roll in the hay, Bat figured. They had been consummating their marriage—before marriage—for some time now. Off in the distance, a guitar, poorly played, was starting up a folk song. The kids were beginning to emerge from their homes; a ball game was shaping up. There weren't many children in New Woodstock, about a hun-

29

dred, but their presence added a needed something, even in an art colony.

They passed Bette and Bea, two models who shared a small mobile home. Bette was taking strenuous exercises. She had formerly been a dancer and made a policy of keeping herself in trim. She had one of the most beautiful complexions Bat had ever seen, being a somewhat light sepia. She was also noted for putting out for any man who asked her to lie down.

Bat said to Ferd, in the way of make-conversation, "Getting any work done?"

Ferd said, virtuously, "Some people might work from sun to sun, but a writer's work is never done."

Bat looked at him from the side of his eyes. "Oh? You don't seem to be wearing yourself to a frazzle."

"I'm working right this very minute," Ferd said, in put-on protest. "One of these days I'll do an article about you. How's this for a title: *Last of the Neighborhood Cops?*"

"It'll never sell. Besides, the word cop is antiquated. They call us pigs, these days. Do you place much of your stuff, Ferd?"

"Some. Not enough to negate my NIT, but some. That's one advantage of NIT, I suppose. Gives somebody who's trying to break into the arts the opportunity to survive while he's learning the tools of his trade."

"No more starving in garrets, eh?" Bat snorted. "I wonder if that starving in garrets didn't have its values so far as the development of art was concerned. It eliminated those who didn't have the necessary push, the gumption, the belief in himself."

Ferd looked over at him. "You sound slightly sour."

Bat shook his head. "Not really. But that's what Di and I were just talking about; NIT, the Meritocracy, the elimination of just about everybody from contributing in society."

They had reached his vehicle and Bat Hardin opened the door and allowed Ferd Zogbaum to precede him.

The Hardin mobile home consisted of a fairly large living room, a mini-kitchen, a bath and a bedroom. In the tradition of house trailers, since their inception, everything was compactly efficient; refrigerator, automatic bar, electronic stove, TV screen, tucked away here and there with a minimum expenditure of space.

Ferd slumped into an easy chair and Bat went over to the bar. "What'll you have?" he said.

"I don't know. What have you got it set up for?"

"Not much, actually. I'm not particularly fancy about my grog. There's pseudo-whiskey, gin, rum, brandy, vermouth, both dry and sweet, tequila, now that we're in Mexico, and the usual mixers."

"It's been a hot day. How about a Cuba Libra?"

"Sounds good to me," Bat said, dialing the rum and coke and a dash of lime juice. He paused a brief moment, then opened the compartment and brought forth two long, chilled plastic glasses. He handed one to Ferd and took a chair himself.

Ferd took up the conversation where they had dropped it. "So what's wrong with the Meritocracy?"

"There's no room for anybody except those with a lot of merit," Bat said wryly.

Ferd sipped his drink and thought about it. "That's not my beef. What it's done is eliminated the democratic ethic."

"Don't say that near any professional propagandist, or he'll wash your mouth out with soap."

"One dollar, one vote," Ferd said. "Some democracy."

"One *earned* dollar, one vote," Bat amended, working

at his own drink. "It does make a difference. Dividends, rents, pension income, income from a trust; none of them count. The slogan is pragmatism. The theory is, the most useful members of society have the most voice in running it."

"Yeah, that's the slogan. And the majority of the citizenry is disenfranchised."

"So when was it different?"

Ferd looked at him and scowled. "How do you mean?"

"Listen, we seem to get into the habit of thinking in labels. Democracy is a label. So far as I'm concerned it's a great idea but there's been precious little of it since primitive times when government was based on the clan and there were few enough people in a society so that all could participate. But take a look at democracy come down through the ages. The great example always given us is the Golden Age of Greece and particularly Athens. But who voted so democratically? The male citizens of Athens. And for every citizen there was a flock of slaves who had no say at all, no matter how intelligent, no matter how productive a member of society. Or bring it down more recently. Did you labor under the illusion that when George Washington's army won their revolution that they were allowed to vote in the new society? They did if they had enough property. Otherwise, they were disenfranchised. Right on down to modern times, it wasn't one man, one vote; there were various ways to keep one whale of a percentage of the population from having their full say. The United States is usually used as an example of all-out democracy, but the slaves weren't freed until 1863, and women weren't given the vote until after the First World War."

Ferd said, a bit on the dogged side, "I get the feel-

32

ing that you're just arguing for the sake of it, that you don't really disagree with me. You're not any more eligible to vote than I am."

Bat chortled and finished his drink. "Man, they had us when they rang the NIT in on us. Obviously, most citizens who had to be subsidized in their income by the State were second-rate citizens. When it started, the so-called floor under everybody's income was at $3,500, the poverty level at that time. Everybody poor enough to have to take the Negative Income Tax was so damn anxious to get it that they'd put up with anything. When the Constitution was rewritten, to fit it in with post-industrial society, there were few to put up a howl about one-dollar-one-vote. They wanted that dole, that security. So now we've got it."

Ferd said, "Yeah, and about ten percent of the population have the vote and of those about three percent, the real ranking members of the Meritocracy, control enough votes to swing any election."

"Well, and isn't the government more efficient and less corrupt than ever before?"

Ferd laughed, a note of deprecation there. "How would I know? It is according to them but they're the ones who control the mass media, the libraries, the schools and all the other means of spreading the good word about themselves. I don't like dictatorship, even a benevolent dictatorship. It's up to the dictators to decide what's benevolent."

Bat was getting tired of the subject. He said, "Another drink?"

"No, I guess not."

Bat said, "What was it that you wanted to see me about, Ferd?"

The other's face worked unhappily for a moment before he answered. He said, "I don't know exactly how to put it, but Bat, something's wrong."

Bat took him in.

Ferd said, "I can't exactly put my finger on it. It's kind of intuitive. But, for one thing, where are the local people?"

"How do you mean?" Bat said, scowling.

He had run into this intuitive feeling of Ferd Zogbaum's before. The other hadn't been with New Woodstock very long but on two occasions he had come up with this intuitive feeling, or whatever it was, and had been astonishingly accurate. That time, for instance, in Colorado when they had parked in an almost dry river bed, strung out along the side of the trickling stream. Ferd, frowning unhappily, as he was frowning now, had suddenly snapped "A cloud burst," although there wasn't much in the way of clouds in the sky. He had been proven right. They had barely gotten the town out of the river bed before the flood was upon them. Two of the mobile homes had been lost, though happily the occupants survived.

Now Ferd said stubbornly, "The last time I was in Mexico, about five years ago, the locals used to hang around the site when a group of American homes came through. Some were there just to gawk, but some had souvenirs and such to sell. Where are they this time?"

Bat scowled again. "Damned if I know. Possibly so many Americans have been coming through that we're no longer a novelty."

Ferd shook his head. "That wouldn't apply to peddlers, or beggars. It especially wouldn't apply to kids. Kids never get tired of gaping at strangers and different ways of doing things."

34

Bat thought about it, biting his lower lip. He said slowly, "Did you notice at the border this morning a, well, kind of a sullen quality about some of the authorities?"

"As a matter of fact, I did. We had all of our papers, permission to enter and all, but I got a distinct feeling that most of them hated to see us pass."

Bat said suddenly, "Look, what do you say we go into town this evening after we eat? Take a look around."

Ferd came to his feet, pulled out his pocket phone and dialed the time. "Okay," he said. "I've got to get back over to Di's now."

"Pick me up here when you're through," Bat said. "I'll have to whomp up my own supper, you lucky jazzer."

Ferd grinned at him. "Virtue is its own reward," he said mockingly.

"And where'll it get you? In the end?" Bat growled back.

After Ferd Zogbaum had gone, Bat went back into his mini-kitchen, opened the refrigerator-freezer and scowled in at the purchases he had made earlier. He wasn't particularly hungry after the heat of the day.

In honor of their first stop in Mexico, he brought forth a container-dish of chili con carne and placed it in the electronic heater and gloomily watched as the container top melted, becoming part of the prepared contents.

The chili con carne heated but the dish remained at room temperature and Bat took the food over to the small table in the living room. From a cabinet he brought forth a set of utensils, some crackers and another plastic of beer and sat down to eat. He wasn't going to need the knife with this meal so he ate it along with the chili.

Come to think of it, he remembered that chili con

35

carne wasn't actually a Mexican dish. Something like chop suey which had been invented by a dishwasher in San Francisco, many years ago, chili con carne was an American version of what the norteamericanos thought the Mexicans *ought* to eat. It had actually been devised in the American border states, probably Texas or Arizona. However, he liked the dish, hearty, filling and flavorful.

When he had finished, he ate the plate and the spoon and fork and went back to his favorite chair to wait for Ferd Zogbaum.

He considered dialing himself an after-dinner drink but decided not to. He had no idea of what they might run into in Linares and didn't want to be even slightly befuddled. He spotted the two plastic glasses he and Ferd had drunk from and got up again to toss them into the sink where they could melt away and go down the drain. Bachelor-like, he hated to have the place cluttered up with dirties.

He reached up for a book from his shelves and sat again. He could have, of course, sat before his library TV screen and dialed practically any book ever published. Long since, the National Data Banks had recorded every volume in the Library of Congress, the British Museum Library and the libraries of every university in the West, all available on his screen for free if the books were on the public domain or at a very nominal sum, automatically deducted from his credit account, if the copyright was still in the hands of the author. However, there was something in Bat Hardin that appreciated the feel of book-in-hand while he was reading. The size of his mobile home prevented him from collecting a large library but he carried with him his favorites, usually to the amusement of visitors to his home.

V

When Bat and Ferd had returned from their disastrous visit to Linares, Ferd had staggered off for his own quarters but Bat got out of his electro-steamer on his side and started over to the colony physician.

Doc Barnes looked startled and came to his feet. "What in the world's happened?" he snapped. And then to his nurse, "Miss Stevens!"

Barbara Stevens hustled to her own feet and held open the door to the colony hospital.

Bat headed into the interior, saying, "Ferd Zogbaum and I went into town and got into trouble at a bar."

Doc Barnes, following him, said grumpily, "I wouldn't think either of you were the types to get into barroom brawls. Here, let me look at that."

They had entered the emergency room and Nurse Stevens, a middle-aged woman, professionally efficient, was going about the necessary tasks to treat the cut.

Bat said, "They were laying for us, Doc. Haven't you noticed the atmosphere?"

"I can't say that I have. Hold still."

"Well, we're evidently not as popular around here as we might be."

The veteran doctor moved briskly, staunched the blood flow, treated the cut, closed it and placed a layer of pseudo-flesh over the wound. "There you are," he said. "Nurse."

Barbara Stevens said, "Lower your pants."

37

Bat looked at her.

She snorted at him and held up the hypodermic she had in hand.

"Oh," he said and obeyed orders.

She gave him the shot in the right hip.

"That'll do it," Doc Barnes said. "It'll be healed in a few days."

"No stitches necessary?" Bat said.

"We don't use them for this sort of thing any more," the older man said. "You going to see Dean about this?"

Bat turned to leave. "I suppose so. I'll have to. Thanks, Doc." His eyes swept the mobile clinic. When on the road, it moved in two sections drawn by two heavy electro-steamers. When parked, and set up, it consisted of two floors, sporting twelve compartments in all, including Doc Barnes' living quarters.

Bat said, "You know, this is one of the best little hospitals I think I've ever seen in a town as small as this."

Doc Barnes said, "You can thank Dean Armanruder and Jim Blake for that. They split the cost fifty-fifty and donated it to the colony."

The doctor looked at Bat narrowly. "You better come into the next room and sit down for a time. A little shock is beginning to set in. Let me see your eyes." He looked closely at the pupils. "I don't think you've got a concussion. You must have a skull as thick as armor plate. What'd he hit you with?" He was leading the way into the adjoining room which served as a waiting room of the clinic during the day hours.

"A baseball bat," Bat growled unhappily. He was feeling slightly nauseated. He suffered Nurse Stevens to help him into an easy chair.

The doctor sat down across from him but the nurse left, evidently to clean up the emergency room.

Bat Hardin said, "Why did they donate this outfit? It must have cost a fortune."

"Contrary to some opinion, these mobile towns are not necessarily solely populated by bums on NIT," Barnes said. "Some people, even well to do people, prefer to live this way. Admittedly, the swanker mobile towns and cities usually exclude anyone not of a certain financial standing but an art colony such as this attracts men like Armanruder and Blake because of the companionship."

"That still doesn't answer my question."

Doc Barnes said impatiently, "They donated it shortly before you joined New Woodstock because I told them I wouldn't take the job unless we had better facilities than were provided at that time."

Bat scowled. "What job? I thought you volunteered your services."

"I do. I'm retired and have all the income I need. Sort of an old workhorse that hates to be out of harness. I saw an advertisement in one of the magazines devoted to mobile town life for a doctor and answered it. New Woodstock's doctor had passed away. Armanruder and Blake liked my qualifications and for the sake of their own selves and family members ponied up the necessary if I'd stay."

"Damn nice of them."

Doc shifted his thin shoulders. "You need a competent general practitioner in a mobile town. It wasn't completely altruistic on their part. They get sick as often as anyone else."

Bat said, "Well, if you wanted to remain in practice, why didn't you stay up north?"

The doctor said testily, "Because I'm outdated. In medicine today you become outdated about every five years. Normally, a competent physician will return to school every five years and spend one or two years catching up on the latest advances. I've got to the age where it's too difficult to keep up. Besides, I like this life. I'm not so confoundedly senile that I don't appreciate a change of scene, open air life, the beach or lakeside in the summer, a southern climate in the winter."

Bat was beginning to feel better but he was in no hurry to go. He liked old Doc Barnes and suspected that the other had been a top man of his field in his day.

He said, "Were all the other auxiliary trailers acquired the same way?"

Doc Barnes squinted at him. "You should know, you've lived in mobile towns before, haven't you?"

"They sometimes differ in how they're composed," Bat said. "The only other one I've lived in was even smaller than this and specialized in archeology. There were precious few auxiliaries, and those largely inadequate, except for the mobile museum. We'd go to archeological digs and set up the town and stay there until the majority wanted to move on to some other archeological site. We were in Yucatan for a while, in the Mayan ruins; very interesting."

"Why did you leave?" Doc said.

Bat shrugged. "For some reason archeological ruins seem to be usually located in grim places. I got tired of heat, mosquitos, inadequate town sites, drab views and abstentminded-scholar types. I decided an art colony would provide more interesting companionship and be inclined to move around in the beauty spots of the continent, instead of parking in jungles, deserts and such. I considered joining up with one of the resort towns, the type that head up for New England or the Canadian Rockies in the summer months and then down to Florida or here to Mexico for the beaches in the winters. But the thing is, those towns are a little too much on the hedonistic side for me. Too much boozing, too much partying. Nobody seems to have much interest in anything but having a good time. Here in New Woodstock almost everybody works at something or at least pretends to. I prefer even a demi-buttocked artist to someone who makes no pretense of doing anything at all except sitting on the beach during the day and getting smashed at a party at night."

The doctor shifted his shoulders again. "I feel the same way. As far as the auxiliaries are concerned, some, such as the ad building and the school, were bought by popular subscription when the town first organized some years ago. Others are privately owned. Sam Prager's TV and electronic repair shop, for instance. Evidently, Sam had always loved to tinker. When his job was automated out from under him, he and his wife, Edith, took what resources they had and made a downpayment on a mobile home and equipped one room as a repair shop."

"I wonder why Sam joined New Woodstock," Bat said. "You'd think he'd look up a town that had a lot of members with similar interests in fiddling around with electronics."

"Edith writes. Poetry, I believe. She's on the striving intellectual side. Answer the question yourself, Bat. Why has a healthy, comparatively young fellow like you retired to a life in New Woodstock?"

Bat told him.

The doctor was irritated. "The word intelligence has its elastic qualities," he said. "The tests we now use are considerably more efficient than they used to be; however, the I.Q. test largely measures the speed of your thinking, not necessarily its quality."

"How do you mean?"

The testy old man said, "See here. Suppose you were shipwrecked on a deserted island. Who would you rather have as a companion, a computer programmer with an I.Q. of 150—gifted, in short—or a chappie with an I.Q. of 110, slightly above average, who was a professional fisherman and spent his vacations in hunting, hiking and skin diving."

Bat said dryly, "These days, you're not apt to be shipwrecked. And under the Meritocracy high I.Q. is the criteria that counts."

The doctor said, "Fast thinking isn't always the best. All chess players of premier standing don't necessarily have high I.Q.s, nor do all top-ranking scientists. Some are pluggers, rather than speed-demon types. In mathematics, for another example, I once studied a boy of twelve who could do problems in his head almost as fast as you could state them. His mind worked at computer speed when it came to multiplication or division. Yet he was just short of being a moron."

"Well, be that as it may, under the Meritocracy you're primarily judged by your I.Q. and evidently on an average the system works. You've really got to operate to buck the system, get a decent education, get a position with one of the major corporations."

Doc Barnes reached over and took Bat's wrist. He said, "Your pulse is all right and you've lost the clammy feeling of shock. I suppose you could go now. One thing

I ought to say to you, Bat, on this low I.Q. thing. You're building up a grand inferiority complex."

Bat Hardin stood and turned to leave. He said, lowly, "It's not an inferiority complex, Doc. I *am* inferior."

VI

Before going to the mobile mansion which was the home of Dean Armanruder, Bat Hardin headed for the considerably less ostentatious home of his deputy, Al Castro.

On the way, he passed the camper of Ferd Zogbaum and considered momentarily sticking his head inside and inquiring about the other's headache. It was a strange thing, that headache. What had Ferd said? That every time he got into a fight the headache hit him.

He approached the other's camper but then drew himself up. Through one of the windows he could see Ferd sitting at his tiny desk talking earnestly into a TV phone. There was a, well, anxious look on his face, one of strain, although he was seemingly trying to control that element of his expression.

Bat shrugged and moved on. Since it seemed unlikely that the freelance writer had any contacts here in Mexico, he must have been communiciating with someone back in the States and the conversation was seemingly of more than passing interest.

Bat shrugged again. For all he knew, Ferd was querying some editor about an article. Possibly the strained element was there because he needed the money. But why should Ferd Zogbaum be hard up for money? He was a single fellow and eligible for his NIT. He could go all year without selling any of his pieces and never be really up against it, particularly since mobile town life

44

was comparatively cheap and Mexico, in particular, considerably less expensive than the States. NIT, these days, was enough that anyone could live-it-up in Mexico or some of the other Latin American countries to the south. And more and more people were discovering the fact every day as witness the exodus of mobile towns and cities southward.

Al Castro's home was approximately the size of Bat's own but since he lived with his well-larded wife, Pamela, the space was really less than he could have wished for. The place was lighted up but the curtains drawn. Bat rang the bell.

Al came, yawning as ever, and opened up.

"Hi, Bat, what's on? Jesus, it's been a hot day. I hate heat. Come on in. Have a drink. Me and the old lady's having a gin and a mixer they call Del Valle down here, based on grapefruit juice. Makes something like a Tom Collins."

Bat followed him into the mobile home.

Pamela Castro was sitting at the small dining-room table, a tall frosted glass there and a wilted look about her. She was an objectionably fat woman and Bat had never particularly got along with her. She couldn't see any reason for her husband donating his time as Bat's deputy when he received no compensation. Theoretically she was a water colorist but in actuality she spent precious little time working at it.

Bat exchanged the usual amenities and turned back to Al Castro wondering all over again how any man could bear having a wife who outweighed him almost two to one and was a couple of inches taller to boot. Well, his wife was one of the few things that Al Castro never seemed to complain about, so evidently she suited him.

45

Bat said, "No thanks. I just had a drink and got knocked for a loop."

"They got strong liquor down here, all right," Al nodded. "But it tastes like turpentine. Take the tobacco stain right off your teeth. I'll stick to State-side grog."

"It wasn't the liquor," Bat said wryly. "It was the bartender. He slugged me with a kid-sized baseball bat."

Al Castro goggled him. "What're you talking about?"

Bat told him what had happened and then, "I'm heading over to see Armanruder but whatever he says I think we'd better post a guard tonight. Why don't you round up a couple of the emergency deputies, say Jake Benton's boy, Tom, and Luke Robertson? We'll share watches, four hours on, four hours off."

"Heavens to Betsy," Pamela complained in a half whine. "Is this getting to be an all day, all night thing? What do you get out of it, up and down all night? You'll be too tired to drive tomorrow."

Al said placatingly, "It's an emergency, honey. You know how seldom we have to guard the town at night."

"That was up in the States," she grumbled. "I bet from now on you'll be doing it every night, with these spics and all."

Al didn't answer that. He turned back to Bat. "Okay, I'll run over and get Tom and Luke. You want we should carry shooters?"

"Good grief, no," Bat told him. "That's all we'd need, is to shoot one of these jokers. We're not even in our own country. They'd stick you in the slammer until you rotted."

"Well, suppose somebody takes a shot at me, first?"

Bat made a gesture of resignation with his hands. "In that case, what can you do? Make a beeline for home and get your own gun, but, oh man, tread carefully. For some

46

reason or other, these people are already down on us. Damn if I can figure out why." He turned to go, saying goodbye over his shoulder to the disgruntled Pamela Castro. She muttered a reply.

Bat made his way across the center area to where Dean Armanruder was set up, not far from the mobile administrative building. The senior member of the executive committee this week had by far the most luxurious mobile home in New Woodstock. His three-section establishment was a far cry from the little trailer homes of the 1930s. Six vehicles in all were involved; three mobile homes which folded quite compactly while underway and three heavy electro-steamers which drew them. Two of the homes were joined, on setting up, to make the quarters which Dean Armanruder and his secretary occupied, and the third home, considerably the smallest, was parked nearby for Manuel Chauvez and his wife, the only two servants in New Woodstock.

Bat Hardin was on friendly enough terms with the retired corporation manager but found no real warmth in the man. In theory, Dean Armanruder dabbled in painting, but in actuality such real professionals as Diana Sward had to repress their shudders if they were unlucky enough to see his latest product.

Armanruder was a phenomenon that has been known to the art colony down through the ages, the outsider who loves to associate with Bohemians—whatever a Bohemian is, Bat thought sourly.

But then again, who was he to talk? He himself, no artist, had come to New Woodstock to enjoy the Bohemian atmosphere and to associate with artists such as Diana Sward and Jim Blake, and aspiring writers such as Ferd Zogbaum. The only difference between him and Dean Armanruder was that he, Bat Hardin, lived on his

47

Negative Income Tax, while Armanruder probably had to pay enough taxes to support a round number of such as Bat Hardin.

The Armanruder home was one of the few in New Woodstock that boasted an identity screen in the door. Bat activated it and stood there waiting for the door to open.

It did and Armanruder's voice came through the screen at the same moment. "Come in, Hardin. Good evening. We're in the salon."

"Good evening," Bat said and entered and made his way down the short corridor to where Dean Armanruder and his secretary, Nadine Paskov, were relaxing before the Tri-Di screen which was built into the end wall of the room, taking up most of it. It was the largest screen in New Woodstock and inwardly Bat Hardin was of the opinion that it was *too* damn large since the Armanruder salon wasn't big enough for you to get far away enough to view it most effectively.

When set up, the mobile mansion had a second floor which telescoped down into the bottom one when underway. The top floor was devoted to sleeping quarters, dressing rooms, closets and baths. Bat had never seen it. The ground floor was living quarters, library, dining room, a surprisingly extensive kitchen for a mobile home, storage space, a large office and a smaller one for Miss Paskov. Nadine Paskov was really a secretary though some snide elements in the colony preferred to doubt that. She also obviously doubled as Dean Armanruder's mistress, and slept around with just about anybody else in New Woodstock who wore pants. She was possibly the most beautiful woman in town, unless Diana Sward held that honor. The difference between Di and Nadine was largely grooming; the latter's every pore was in place and the former always looked like a slob so far as make-up and dress were concerned. However, for his money Bat Hardin would take the artist any day.

Dean Armanruder touched a control on the arm of his overgrown chair and the lights went up sufficiently for them to see each other with more ease.

"Sit down, Hardin," he said. "Could I have Manuel bring you a drink?" He touched another control.

That was the Armanruder style. No automatic bar for him nor even an old-fashioned one which he would have to operate himself. Of course not. When he wanted a drink he didn't stir from his chair, even though the beverage in question was only a half-dozen steps away. No, he summoned Manuel who was seemingly on duty twenty-four hours a day and could really rest only when his boss was asleep.

Cool it, cool it, Bat told himself. What business of his was it? Armanruder had earned his comforts. You didn't become manager of a corporation these days because your father owned most of the stock. The wealthy might inherit a concern but few were foolish enough to attempt to operate it themselves. If they did there was a good chance of disaster. You won to the top these days through merit. Armanruder obviously had plenty of it, the type of merit that counted in their ultra-competitive society.

Bat took a chair but said, "No thanks. I'm going to be up half the night and a drink would probably make me that much more groggy." He nodded to Nadine Paskov, ever the beauty queen, who this evening wore one of the new Cretan Revival gowns, the breasts bared, the nipples painted red. She looked as though bored by his arrival. He said, "Good evening, Miss Paskov."

"Hi Bat," she said, disinterestedly. She finished the drink in her highball glass.

Manuel entered but for the moment Dean Armanruder ignored him. The small, dark-complexioned servant wore a white jacket now. During the day, while driving one of the Armanruder units, he wore a dark suit and a chauffeur's cap.

Armanruder said to Bat, "How do you mean, you'll be up tonight?"

Bat told him the day's developments and the older man was obviously disturbed. "Why in the world did you two have to go into town?"

"I told you that. We sensed a sullen quality and wanted to check up on it. We certainly weren't looking for trouble and would have avoided it if we could."

"From what you said, that ne'er-do-well, young Zogbaum, precipitated the fight."

"Not really. You could feel it in the air. Had we known, of course, we wouldn't have gone into town. But we didn't. I don't think it's too important, especially since we'll be pulling out tomorrow. Nevertheless, it won't hurt for a couple of us to patrol the town tonight."

"I suppose so," the other said, then looked at his butler cum chauffeur. "Two more of the same for Miss Paskov and me, Manuel. Mr. Hardin isn't drinking."

"Yes, sir." The Spanish American turned to go. If Bat had it correctly, Manuel and his wife, Concha, had come from New Mexico or Arizona. Their Spanish would be invaluable on this move down to South America.

Bat looked after the slightly built servant and must have had an element of questioning on his face.

Dean Armanruder misunderstood it. He said, "You're wondering why Manuel would take a job like this in these days of NIT? It's a fact that servants are few indeed in

50

the States any more. Only the truly wealthy can afford them. But it's not that with Manuel and Concha; I pay them little more than they would get in the way of NIT."

Bat Hardin was mildly surprised at the other. What business was it of Bat's?

Armanruder chuckled and said, "Poor Manuel is over a barrel. He's not eligible for NIT."

"Oh? I was under the impression that he was an American citizen."

Armanruder chuckled again. "Yes. But not all citizens are eligible for NIT. You see, friend Manuel was caught at falsifying his income tax. He and his wife were collecting their NIT but working on the side to augment their fortunes. Very, very bad. When the computers check you out and catch you, you're no longer eligible for NIT and in this day and age of unemployment you have your work cut out finding a position."

Bat said, "Actually, that wasn't what I was thinking, though. The thought went through my mind, there but for luck go you or I."

Nadine Paskov said in bored impatience, "Oh, good heavens."

But Armanruder shook his head. "Speak for yourself, perhaps, Hardin, but not for me. Luck is not involved. Manuel Chauvez and I come from different strata in society. It was fated that he occupy his position and I, mine. At his birth he was slated to be a servant or the equivalent, I to be among the top one percent of our system."

He settled back in his chair, made a dome of his fingers and his tone became slightly pompous. "The fact of the matter is, Hardin, that our present Meritocracy doesn't differ as much as all that from previous socio-

51

economic systems. Down through recorded history the real developments of the human race have been made by about one percent of the population.

"Discoveries, inventions, breakthroughs, new arts and sciences, the things that count in the advancing of the race. Under all social systems, not just Meritocracy, the elite came to the top and directed, planned or developed."

Bat was feeling perverse. He said sourly, "Or, at least, they could claim they were and who was in a position to argue?"

The older man shook a finger at him negatively. "No, you're incorrect. Hardin, the human race has been on Earth for something like a million years. Up until about eight thousand years ago it progressed very slowly indeed under a system of what you might call primitive communism, community ownership of such property as existed and largely democratic institutions based on family and clan. It wasn't until the advent of class divided society and private ownership of the means of production that the race began to forge ahead. Obviously, no single person invented the institution of chattel slavery but if one had he should have been listed as one of the greatest benefactors the race has had."

Bat Hardin's eyebrows went up but he let the other proceed.

Armanruder went on pontifically. "If anyone was to have the leisure time—leisure from primary labor, that is—to develop the sciences and arts, it meant that the overwhelming majority of people in a society must sacrifice themselves so that a small minority could be free. Say, five percent of the population. And that five percent must be the elite, and was. But even among them, the slave-owning class, only about one percent made the great advances."

"Once again," Bat said dryly, "how do you know they were really elite, that they had the best brains and abilities?"

The former corporation manager shook his finger again. "Because if they weren't, the true elite emerged and displaced them."

"Always?"

"Always. Under the older socio-economic systems, slavery, feudalism, classical capitalism, it might take time, but sooner or later those with the true abilities took command." He thought about it for a moment, then added, "Admittedly, it sometimes took quite a while to depose the incapable and you usually had to shoot them out. No ruling class or caste will give up its position of power and wealth without resistance. That's one point where the Meritocracy is superior over past systems."

"How do you mean?" Bat said. He was antagonized by the other's pomposity but the subject fascinated him, since it struck so near to home.

The older man said, "Under the Meritocracy you seek and reach your level. It's a system that fits the human race because it's one that is stratified, because people are. It's a highly disciplined society, as the universe is. It's a society in which individuals can freely move from one level to another but only by their own abilities. Nothing counts except your own individual achievements."

"Oh, Lord, all this is boring me spitless," Nadine Paskov said.

Bat Hardin came to his feet. He had a few arguments in his mind but he said, "I should be getting on my rounds." He added wryly, "I suppose the manner in which we do the little governing that is needed in these mobile towns is the last of the old time democracy."

Armanruder chuckled. "Yes. And do you see who our fellow townsmen elected to the executive committee? We who, before retirement, were most successful in our positions in society. You don't find men like your impetuous friend Zogbaum on the executive committee."

VII

As Bat Hardin walked back to his own home, with the intention of getting a little sleep before relieving Al Castro, he muttered, "No. And you don't see me on the executive committee either."

It came to him that high intelligence wasn't the only requirement to get to the top in this each-man-for-him-self-and-the-devil-take-the-hindmost world. You had to have the push and aggression of a Dean Armanruder. A lazy genius isn't one. When Armanruder had first come to the mobile art colony, he had begun operating, volunteering his services, taking over responsibilities. Most of the town's members did a minimum of participating in its required community work. Oh, there were few complete shirkers but the average citizen was too taken up with his art work, his family, the maintenance of his mobile home, to find time for lengthy committee meetings, the handling of accounts, the making of decisions involving the community.

Within a month, Dean Armanruder had been elected to the executive committee and within two months was dominating it. Not that Bat Hardin was complaining. The other was efficient, intelligent, farseeing. It was seldom that he took a stand with which Bat disagreed. Had New Woodstock been under a town manager, as was the case with many of the larger mobile towns and cities, Bat's vote would have gone for Dean Armanruder.

He relieved Al Castro at ten o'clock and patrolled the

55

town with Luke Robertson, a tall, lanky, slow-moving fellow who did sculpturing in iron and who seemed to have an inordinate affection for Bat Hardin, as did his wife, for that matter. Bat wasn't quite sure why. But when somebody likes you, for whatever reason, you have a tendency to like him in return. In actuality, Bat had to admit that he didn't appreciate Luke's work, in fact, it was exactly the sort of abstract, meaningless—to Bat Hardin—sort of thing that he actively disliked. Bat's tastes went to the representational art forms, even free verse left him with a taste in his mouth. Of course, he had never mentioned that to Luke Robertson.

Al Castro and young Tom Benton had reported their four-hour watch uneventful. They had immediately—Al yawning mightily—taken off for their respective homes as soon as their relief had taken over.

The hours between ten and two were equally free of any signs of disgruntled locals. In fact, Bat was beginning to wonder if he hadn't made a fool of himself by taking these precautions.

Al and Tom relieved him and Luke again at two, and having copied Al's contagious yawn, Bat made his way back to his trailer. In the living room, he scowled momentarily at his bar. But no, the hell with it. Tomorrow was going to be one long day and he couldn't afford to be even a bit woozy.

He turned out the light and began unbuttoning his shirt as he made his way back to the bedroom.

56

VIII

At dawn, Bat made a sudden decision. He checked the power packs which he had charged during the night, activated the car and started up. He picked up his phone and said, "New Woodstock, Dean Armanruder."

But it was Nadine Paskov's face which faded onto the screen. She was obviously in bed and for once the glamorous secretary was less than her best, even though she slept nude and was bare to her waist.

She looked at him sleepily—and indignantly—and said, "What in the damn world do you want at this time of the damned night?"

Bat said mildly, "Sorry. I wanted to let Mr. Armanruder know I was going to take a quick scout along the route we're taking today. I assume that I'll be back before the town takes off. If not, I'll rejoin along the route.

"I couldn't care less," she said snippishly and making with a yawn that would have done credit to Al Castro, the expert.

"Please tell Mr. Armanruder," Bat said. "Sorry again."

She muttered something nasty and flicked off.

It wasn't necessary to enter Linares proper to continue on along the highway, for which Bat Hardin was thankful, although he rather doubted the town would be awake this early. Mexicans are seldom early risers he had found out from his previous visits. Perhaps it went back to the old days when they were without means of heat-

57

ing their homes and remained in bed until the sun had warmed the world.

He drove along Route E-60, the road rather rapidly ascending. It was considerably more beautiful a drive than had been the day before with its flatness of countryside; however, Bat wasn't particularly observant of scenic values. He still had his premonitions and chewed away at his heavy lower lip as he drove. There didn't truly seem to be anything untoward. But . . .

He sped along at a clip of two hundred kilometers an hour. He wasn't in too much of a hurry. He didn't expect to go any further than the Pan American Highway and he'd make that in half an hour or so; however, he wanted to be sure and be back to New Woodstock before the town took off past Linares.

They nailed him about five kilometers before he reached the tiny hamlet of Iturbide and about forty kilometers out of Linares. There was a road block of three cars, only one of which was a steamer and it an old-fashioned kerosene burner, by the looks of it.

Four men, two of them in a uniform which Bat didn't place and all of them armed, stood before the road block.

Bat came to a halt and activated the window.

One of the civilian-dressed of the four came over and said, "Senor Hardin? Come out, please." His English was at least as good as Bat's own.

Bat opened the door and came forth, scowling. He said, "How did you know my name?" His eyes went over them. The alleged uniforms were obviously makeshift. He snapped, "You're not police!" and his hand shot for his shoulder holster.

Bat Hardin was not slow at the draw, but the Mexican was a blur. His own pistol was out and trained on the American's stomach.

58

He said softly, "Move much more slowly, Senor Hardin, and give me that for which you were reaching. So. You carry a gun here in Mexico. To shoot Mexicans with, undoubtedly."

Bat brought forth the gun and handed it over. He said, "I have a permit issued by your border authorities. Our town is going all the way down. At least to Peru. Undoubtedly we'll be going through some fairly wild country in places like Colombia and Ecuador. So we have various guns. They weren't meant to be used against the citizens of your charming country."

He submitted to a frisk by the other, who relieved him of his pocket phone.

The Mexican stuck Bat's Gyro-jet pistol in his belt and said, "You'll never reach Peru or Ecuador, Senor Hardin, which will undoubtedly be a great relief to them. This way, please." He indicated with his gun the more modern of the three cars.

"Where do you think you're taking me?"

"It is not a matter of mere thinking, Senor Hardin. Just to make matters clear, I would not particularly mind shooting you, although this is not the purpose of your, ah, arrest."

Bat climbed into the seat next to that of the driver. Into the back climbed one of the uniformed men, a short carbine at the ready and trained at the back of the American's head.

The English-speaking one took the driver's seat and started up. They had to wait a half minute for the engine to heat, the steamer being that old a model.

"What am I supposed to have done?" Bat demanded.

"Nothing in particular, simply being a gringo here in Mexico."

"Who are you people?"

59

The other ignored him and said something in Spanish to the Mexican in the rear. That one threw what seemed to be a towel over Bat's eyes and tied it roughly. Bat winced when the cut on the side of his head had pressure applied to it.

They drove only a few minutes before taking off on what was obviously a side road. A side road to the right, Bat remembered. He might have to remember such information in the future. He hadn't the vaguest idea of what he was up against. They went on for what he estimated to be two kilometers, climbing rather steeply, if Bat, in his blindfold, could estimate correctly.

Finally they came to a halt and car doors opened. There were other voices now, in the background, all speaking Spanish. Bat was taken by each arm, not especially roughly, and led forward.

"Watch your step," the English-speaking one said.

"Watch your own," Bat rasped. "You people realize that you're kidnapping an American citizen?"

There was a chuckle but he couldn't tell from whom it came.

The one with whom he had been carrying on the conversation said, amusement in his voice, and something more, "We do indeed, Senor Hardin."

They entered a house, led him down what was evidently a hall. He tried to count the steps he took, so as to be able to identify the house later. They obviously entered a room and then sat him in a chair.

A new voice, an older voice and a highly cultured one, said, "Ah, Mr. Hardin. You do not look like a villain, Mr. Hardin. But I suppose you do not know that you are a villain. Villains seldom think of themselves as villains, so I understand. They usually think they are being terribly put upon by their victims and only doing what is correct."

Bat snapped, "What is the meaning of all this? I don't have the vaguest idea of why you have grabbed me, or what's going on. How do you know my name?"

"That is not important, Mr. Hardin, and we are not particularly interested in you. Any of your town authorities, or even an ordinary member of your community would have done. It is just that circumstances made it you, rather than someone else. We wish to issue an ultimatum."

"An ultimatum!" Bat snapped. "I'm beginning to suspect that you're all around the bend. What was the idea of stopping me, dressed in those phony uniforms? You're not Mexican officials; certainly you're not police."

"But we *are* Mexicans, Mr. Hardin, and in a way even police. Vigilante police. And here is our ultimatum. Your mobile town of New Woodstock must turn about and return to your own country."

Had Bat Hardin not been blindfolded, he would have stared.

The speaker said flatly, "We do not want you here in Mexico, Mr. Hardin."

"Who are you?" Bat demanded.

"We are Mexicans," the other said, more emotion in the elderly voice. "Mexicans who are tired of having their country raped by you endless hordes of norteamericanos."

Bat said hotly, "We applied for and received all permissions required by the Mexican authorities to pass through the country and exit through Guatemala."

"We do not agree with some of our authorities. They are overly conscious of the American dollars spent by your tourists, your vacationists and you who permanently establish yourselves in our country and devastate it. You corrupt our young people with your money, your lack of moral decency, your arrogance to a proud people, your pretense to a superior culture."

Bat began to say something but the older man interrupted him. "When I was a boy, you used to cross the border in ones and twos, some as ordinary tourists, some in their house trailers. We welcomed you, welcomed the dollars you spent in our country. It must have been at the time of the 1969 Olympics that the dam first broke. That year not scores or even hundreds of your trailers and mobile homes crossed but literally thousands. And that was just the beginning. When you established your fantastic Negative Income Tax and millions of your people were suddenly free to leave America's overcrowded cities with their slums and ghettos, then they swarmed out over not only your own land but Canada and, above all, Mexico as well."

A new voice, a younger voice but still in English added, "And now my own country, Guatemala, and the other nations to the south. Everywhere, everywhere, your damnable mobile cities destroy the countries in which they park."

"Listen," Bat said. "We pay our way. We spend plenty in every country we go through or remain in. Your people benefit by the dollars we spend."

The older man's voice same again. "A few benefit. Most of us, not at all. Our way of life, our culture, is destroyed. The sites in which you stay, government built, are government operated. It collects for the power you buy, it collects for the expenditures you make in the ultra-markets, restaurants and cantinas located on each site. Admittedly, the money realized is used by our authorities in their grandiose attempts to speed up the industrialization of Mexico. But some of us are not even sure that we wish to be industrialized to the fantastic extent to which you of the north have accomplished."

Bat began to retort, but the other overrode him.

He said, "Mr. Hardin, Mexico's relationship with the colossus to the north has not been a happy one, by and large. Do you labor under the illusion that Texas was liberated—I believe that is the tongue-in-cheek term— by Texans? Such men as Davy Crockett and Jim Bowie were not Texans, Mr. Hardin, they were, ah, volunteers from the United States, adventurers come to wrest wealth from a weaker people. The flag that flew over the Alamo and was captured by Santa Anna's army was that of a volunteer troop from New Orleans. And did you know, Mr. Hardin, the big reason the Texan revolt took place? Most of the American immigrants were from your southern states and couldn't bear the fact that Mexico had abolished slavery. But Texas was not enough. Border trouble was provoked and what are now your states of Arizona, New Mexico, California and parts of others were also seized. The fact that the seizure was premeditated is to be seen in the fact that your General Fremont and his army had trekked all the way to California before the war was declared and was ready at hand to capture that area.

"It was not the last time that you invaded our country, Mr. Hardin. Time and again you crossed our borders when what you deemed were your interests were threatened, when we elected a president of whom you didn't approve, or when our internal policies didn't coincide with your desires.

"But all that is past history. It is the present to which we object. Your New Woodstock is but a small town,

63

comparatively. Your mobile cities come and completely dominate our country. The best beaches from Tijuana to the Guatemala border and from Matamoros to Yucatan are crowded with them. Manzanilla, for instance, once a small fishing town and resort, now has no room for Mexicans on vacation. Thousands upon thousands of your luxurious mobile homes cover every desirable spot. Every restaurant is full of your people, every bar, every nightclub overruns with them.

"Nor is it simply the beaches. Every scenic area in Mexico knows your mobile towns and cities. Lakes Potscuaro and Chapala have been ruined, a Mexican cannot get within a half mile of either. Your hordes eat up the best products of our seas and our fields and orchards. With your fantastic incomes, you shame a Mexican, make him appear a beggar in comparison. In such resorts you run up the prices astronomically so that we can no longer buy even mildly luxurious items."

The older-sounding man snorted in contempt. "What is your current Per Capita Annual Income? Something like $20,000?"

Bat said sourly, "Precious few of we who live in mobile towns have incomes approaching that."

"But nevertheless, even a comparatively well-to-do Mexican seldom sees the amount one of your people gets in what you call NIT."

Bat said angrily, "If you people would cool your population explosion a little your Per Capita Income would go up too. Your population increases almost as fast as your industrialization."

The first voice he had heard, that of the leader of the group that had captured him spoke then and bitterly. "We do not need lessons in the manner in which to control the size of our families, Senor Hardin. One of our greatest objections to your presence is the manner in which you spread your corrupt moral code. Your young men seduce our most beautiful girls with their wealth; seldom do they marry them. But when they do marry, it is usually to girls of our better families who cannot resist the affluence offered them. Your own women are shameless whores, often in your towns running about in their top-less styles. Their sexual code is like that of a bitch in heat."

The old voice came again. "Nor is that the only manner in which you destroy our culture. Supposedly you of the most advanced nations—speaking in terms of Gross National Product—are interested in developing we smaller countries. In actuality, you smother us. Your capital dominates our mines, our best fields, our backward industries. The oil and iron of Venezuela do not belong to Venezuelans, for example; it belongs to norteamericanos, and that is but one example. But even that is not all. How can our people get underway when the intellectual drain bleeds us white of our best minds and most highly trained technicians? My own son is a surgeon. Does he operate on his people who need him so badly? No, he has been attracted by the high pay in the United States."

A new voice broke in, as bitter as were the others. "But your towns, your hundreds of thousands of mobile homes, streaming south. It is they that blanket our country, and, in continuing contact with your people, make us envious of your affluence and susceptible to your corruption. Why, even this New Temple that sweeps your country—it is a religion of no religion. What do you think our simpler people are to believe when they see that such a religion is that of a people who live like gods by their standards?"

Bat said, "Listen. None of this is deliberate on our part. It began a long time ago and accelerated and there is no way to call a halt. We Americans have a tradition of being on the move. Our ancestors had it in their blood when they came over in leaky ships, largely from Europe. They had it when they pressed ever west in the wagon trains, the mobile homes of that day. When the house trailers began to emerge in the 1920s, after the advent of the automobile, we took to them overnight. By the 1960s, fifteen percent of all homes built in the States were mobile homes. And that was only the beginning. When the guaranteed annual wage came along, the multitude of unhappy dwellers in the slums and ghettos were able to make an exodus from them. They swarmed out of the large cities and millions of them took to the mobile home life."

"But why inflict yourselves on us?" someone barked.

Bat looked in that direction. "It was a natural development. When the mobile homes began to merge into mobile cities, sites were set up all over America for them. In the national parks, in the mountains, along the beaches, in the more picturesque deserts even. In a way it was a partial answer to the population growth. Large areas of the country had been going to waste, as far as living room was concerned. There had been a trend toward crowding ever more into the largest cities, with all the problems that were involved such as pollution, smog, parking, traffic, and a dozen more. But with the mobile cities, they could move out into the west, into areas where there was plenty of room."

"But why Mexico! Gringos go home! You're destroying our country. We don't want you!"

Bat said stubbornly, "Your officials gave us permission to enter."

"Yes, our officials! Your dollars corrupt everything. Our officials cannot see beyond the immediate millions that accrue to them through the money you spend."

"We're only passing through," Bat said. "We'll only be in Mexico for a short time. We're heading all the way down the Pan American Highway to South America."

The voice of the one from Guatemala broke in heatedly. "Yes, and in our small country your presence is even more objectionable. We of the more progressive classes are up in arms. I have come all this way to join the forces of Don Caesar——"

"Shuush," somebody muttered.

". . . and to prevent you from going any further. Why some of your towns are already swarming over nations as far south as Chile and the Argentine. Why you have not already been met with arms I cannot say."

Bat said impatiently, "Why pick on New Woodstock? I've never heard of anything like this before. You haven't attempted to turn back other towns."

The older man's voice said, "Quite deliberately, Mr. Hardin. Obviously, what we do is illegal by Mexican law. However, we are dedicated and determined men. You will be an example. The fact that you are a mobile art colony, with all the connotations that brings to the average person's mind, will make the example stronger. Were we to attempt to stop a city or town composed almost entirely of elderly retirees, it would be more difficult for us to gain sympathy both in your own country and ours. But an art colony has a connotation of Bohemian life, immoral artists, wild parties, much drinking of alcohol and smoking of marijuana."

Bat said bitterly, "You'd be surprised how hard working and staid most real artists are."

"That is beside the point. It will be what people think,

not the reality. Those that support us will draw a vivid picture of the depravity of New Woodstock, Mr. Hardin, and how God-fearing, country-loving Mexicans turned you back in indignation."

"And if we don't turn back?"

"We are dedicated and determined men, Mr. Hardin."

"I suspect you're just a handful of malcontents. The majority of Mexicans don't support your views."

"It hasn't been put to a vote, gringo," his original captor said. "However, there's more of us than you would think. All right, the ultimatum has been served. What is your answer?"

"It isn't up to me," Bat said flatly. "New Woodstock is operated democratically. It'll have to be brought before the executive committee."

"Very well," the old man said. "José, return him to his car."

José, evidently the original captor, spoke rapidly in Spanish for a moment, then took Bat by the arm. "Let's go, gringo," he said.

Bat came to his feet and suffered the other to lead him back the way they had come earlier. They retraced the route in the same elderly steamer and the blindfold was not removed until they reached the spot where Bat's car had been left. They kept him carefully covered.

José looked into the interior of the car thoughtfully. He reached out with the barrel of the revolver he carried —it was an old-style, possibly World War Two vintage, six-shooter—and smashed the screen of the vehicle's phone.

"Hey, that was a dirty trick," Bat protested.

José said apologetically, "Sorry. We'd rather you not be able to communicate with the police immediately."

"I'll do just that when I get back to Linares."

"That will give us time enough."

"How about my gun?"

"I'll keep your gun, Senor Hardin. "I'd hate to have you using it on me, later."

"I told you our guns were not to be used against the citizens of this country."

The other's voice was dry. "That remains to be seen, gringo."

Bat climbed into the car, started it up and made a wide turn, heading back for the site where New Woodstock had settled for the previous night.

He swore under his breath. He supposed he could have asked the Mexican to return his pocket TV phone but on the face of it the other wouldn't have for the same reason he had broken the electro-steamer's phone. It was going to be a hassle to get another pocket phone here in Mexico. He'd probably have to wait until he got to Mexico City and the American Consulate. These days, the unique device combined not only a portable TV phone, but your identity number which embraced your credit card, your voter's registration, your military number, what amounted to your post office box, your income tax registration, and everything else in the way of identity, including passport.

Well, it couldn't be helped.

New Woodstock was beginning to get itself together preparatory to leaving, when Bat arrived. However, it would undoubtedly take a couple of hours or so more before it was really ready to roll. Instead of going to see Dean Armanruder immediately, he returned to his home with a cup of coffee in mind. He wanted to think about it a little before confronting the executive committee's questions. Obviously, they would depend largely on his opinions and Bat Hardin wasn't quite sure what they were.

He entered his mobile home and stared at the table. His pocket phone cum credit card was on it.

He took it up, still gaping disbelief. So far as he could see, there was nothing wrong with it. He said into it, "New Woodstock, Al Castro."

Al Castro yawned at him but on this occasion it was not simply a mannerism. He was still in bed. "Hi, Bat. What's up?"

"Sorry," Bat said. "I was just testing my phone. Forgot you'd be sleeping."

"My pal," Al yawned, fading off.

Bat left his home and looked up and down. Sam Prager's mobile home and electronic repair shop was parked next to him on one side but nobody seemed to be about his place. Probably still in bed. The Pragers were inclined to read late into the night and arise at a late hour.

Ferd Zogbaum's camper was on the other side but there was no sign of Ferd. Bat strode over in that direction and ran into his comrade on the far side of the camper. He was evidently deep in a heated discussion with Jeff Smith, a discussion that was already just short of physical violence by the looks of it. Not that Bat had any illusions about the possible outcome. Ferd had size on the feisty southerner, and, besides that, Bat hadn't missed the professional pugilist shuffle the other had gone into the night before.

Smith was saying, his voice shaking with rage, "All right, I've told you, Zogbaum, stay away from her."

Ferd said, only slightly less violently, "And I tell you, Smith, that all this is up to Diana. To her and to me.

She'll associate with whoever the hell she wants to associate with. You're not her husband."

"All right," Smith snapped. "You asked for it!" He began to fall into a fighter's stance. At least, Bat decided, the little man had guts.

Bat began, "Okay, okay, you two. Break it up, you're not a couple of kids."

Jeff turned on him, glowering. "Shut up, *nigger.*"

IX

Bat stared at Jeff Smith for a moment, then threw back his head and laughed.

"I'll be damned," he said. "It's been a long time since I've heard that word. I thought it was out of date. You must be the last of the old-time Southerners. As a matter of fact, my maternal grandmother was a Black, but I doubt if even she was full-blooded. In this day and age there are precious few full-blooded Blacks in the United States except for that small number of recent immigrants from Africa."

"Any nigger blood at all makes you a nigger, nigger."

Bat grinned at him. "So I understand was the law in some of the southern states in the old days. Your name is Smith, eh? Probably British descent. Did it ever occur to you, Smith, that the Romans never drew the color line? Some of the emperors, even, were Africans."

"What's that got to do with it?" Smith snapped.

"The Romans never drew the color line and they occupied England for half a millennium. How can you be sure that you are as lily-white a Caucasian as all that? Are you sure none of your ancestors didn't marry one of those Romans who'd been touched with the tar brush?" Bat laughed his contempt.

"Why, you black bastard."

Ferd Zogbaum, as disgusted as his friend was, growled, "As far as that goes, Bat's complexion isn't much darker than your own."

72

"Keep out of it, Zogbaum," Smith snapped. It was hard to tell, at this point, who his primary antagonist was.

Bat said, conversationally, "For that matter, I wonder just what percentage of your Southerners have African blood in them. For two centuries and more you had your black slaves. For all that time, your men forced themselves on the more attractive girls. What was the old saying among your young fellows? You're not a man until you've had a nigger? And don't forget the old custom in towns like New Orleans where young aristocrats set up apartments in the French Quarter for their quadroon or octaroon mistresses. You know what the children of an octaroon look like, Smith? They look white and they move to another town and pass as white. Did you labor under the illusion that the famed Creole beauties of Louisiana were solely of French descent?"

Bat was suddenly fed up with the argument and with himself for bothering to get into it. He turned to Ferd and said, "Could I talk to you a minute? It's important."

"Sure, why not?" Ferd said, ignoring Jeff Smith. He took Bat's arm and headed around the camper, leaving the feisty smaller man to glare after them.

Bat said, when they were out of earshot, "What was all that?"

Ferd shrugged it off. "Christ only knows. Evidently, Jeff has delusions of being a great lover, or something. He's got a thing—wants to lay Diana so bad, he can taste it. She wouldn't get into bed with him on a bet."

"Well, I don't blame him. She a darn nice girl and a damn beautiful one."

"Sure. But unfortunately for Jeff, she doesn't have a thing for him. What'd you want to see me about?"

"Did you see anybody go into my trailer this morning while I was gone?"

73

"I didn't even know you were gone, but no. Something stolen, or something? We don't have much in the way of petty thievery around New Woodstock. I'd hate to see it start."

"Not that. As a matter of fact, it's the other way. Somebody put something back."

Ferd took him in, and Bat made a quick rundown of the morning's happenings, including the return of the pocket phone.

Ferd hissed a whistle.

Bat said, "In actuality, it was damned decent of them to return it. They didn't have to and there must have been some risk involved. These vigilantes aren't really bad people and in a way I can see their beef."

"Sure. Great," Ferd said in deprecation. "But that's not going to do you much good when they start sniping away at us from the top of some hill as we go driving by."

Bat said, "Well, keep it under your hat for the time being. I'll see what Dean Armanruder has to say first, and then we'll have to bring it up before the executive committee."

Bat stood before the identity screen of the Armanruder home and activated it.

Nadine Paskov's voice said impatiently, "You again? I thought you said you were driving up the road to check it."

Bat said patiently, "I'm back. I'd like to see Mr. Armanruder."

"He's having his breakfast."

"It's of the greatest importance, Miss Paskov."

"Just a minute."

Within that time the door opened and Bat stepped

through and started down the corridor to the dining room.

"Good morning, Hardin," the retired magnate said, looking up from his meal. "Coffee? Sit down."

Nadine Paskov wasn't present but a dirty cup and plate indicated where she had taken her own breakfast. The Armanruder establishment was one of the few in New Woodstock that didn't utilize disposable plates and utensils but, then, it was also the only home that had servants to clean up.

Bat accepted the coffee and launched into his story. By the time he had finished, Dean Armanruder was bug-eyeing him.

He banged his cup down, came to his feet and said, "Come with me," and led the way to his office.

He sat at his desk and activated the TV phone screen. "The police station in Linares," he snapped.

A Mexican face faded in.

Armanruder snapped, "Do you speak English?"

The other said evenly, "For all practical purposes, all educated Mexicans speak English. It is currently a required subject in our institutions of higher learning. May I ask who you are and what you wish?"

"I am Dean Armanruder, senior member of the executive committee of the mobile town of New Woodstock. I might add that I have had the pleasure of attending various business and social functions with the president of your country. We have many mutual friends and associates."

The other didn't seem overly impressed. He said, "And I am Miguel Avila DeLeon, captain of police of the city of Linares. What can I do for you, Senor?"

"This morning our town patrolman, Bat Hardin, was kidnapped by armed men on the road to San Roberto.

He was forced to accompany them to some spot where he was confronted by a group that demanded New Woodstock turn back to the United States."

The captain of Mexican police frowned disbelief but said courteously, "Who were these men?"

Bat came over and stood next to Armanruder. "I wouldn't know. I was blindfolded. However, one who was obviously an older man was addressed as Don Caesar and the one who kidnapped me was called José."

"Both rather common names in Latin countries," the captain said. "They turned you loose?"

"Yes, of course, here I am."

"Unharmed?"

Bat took a deep breath. "Yes."

The captain had a few other questions as to where the kidnapping had taken place, whether or not anything had been taken from the American, or if he had in any manner been injured. Bat aswered everything to the best of his ability but there seemed to be a strange something in the police head's manner.

Finally it came out. He said, "Senor Hardin, if I am not mistaken you are the gentleman who, in company with another Norteamericano, provoked a drunken brawl—"

"We weren't drunk!"

Captain DeLeon went on, ". . . in one of the cantinas here in Linares, severely battering several of the citizens. My men took measures to see that none of your victims carried the matter further but it would seem that some of them, working behind our backs, took their revenge by playing a bit of a prank on you."

Bat said flatly, "The men who kidnapped me had no relationship to those in the bar. My kidnappers were

76

educated men who spoke excellent English. Those in the bar were town bums."

"I am sure you are mistaken, Senor Hardin, however, I will look into the matter."

Armanruder said harshly, "What are you going to do about it?"

The captain shrugged a most Latin shrug and pursed his lips in regret. "I doubt if there is anything I can do about it, but, as I say, I shall investigate. Have you decided to turn back?"

"No, we haven't!" Armanruder snapped, flicking off the set.

He sat and glared in Bat's direction, but not at him.

Bat said musingly, "The captain's voice. I've heard it before, or, at least, I think I have. It was one of the voices when I was blindfolded."

"Are you sure?"

"No, not sure, but I think it was."

Dean Armanruder steamed for a moment, then flicked on the set again. He said, "John Fielding, President of United Mobile Cities Association of America, New Denver, Colorado."

When the face came in, it was an impatient face. "Fielding here. I must say, this is an untoward hour. I won't be in my office until nine."

Armanruder said, just as snappishly, "And this is an untoward situation." He gave Bat's story to the association head in detail.

The other thought about it unhappily. He took a deep breath finally and said, "This is the worst yet."

"You mean there have been other examples?"

"Mr. Armanruder, do you know how many mobile cities, towns and villages crossed the border yesterday?

Twenty-two, including New Woodstock. The largest was a city of more than fifty thousand occupants. Of course, this is the high season. Most of these mobile towns will remain in Mexico for only a few weeks, or months, but some plan to remain indefinitely. The number increases each year. Wouldn't you expect a certain amount of friction?"

"Friction isn't quite the way to put it. These men were heavily armed. They threatened Mr. Hardin's life."

John Fielding nodded. "I suspect that before we're through it will continue to get worse. We've had negative reports even from Common Europe. These new bulk carriers will ferry a mobile home across the Atlantic for as little as a hundred dollars. Already, whole towns are going over to Spain, Italy and Greece, in particular. The Italians are considering laws to curb them, but merchants and other elements that profit by tourism are resisting."

Dean Armanruder said, "What are you going to do?"

"About Mr. Hardin's adventure? What can we do? We'll protest to the Mexican tourism authorities but, actually, you have very little in the way of evidence to present and evidently aren't getting much in the way of support from the local police in acquiring more. Frankly, I'm inclined to think it a bluff. A small number of malcontents who wished to throw a scare into you. The moment one of them actually fired a shot, the Mexican police would be on them like a flash."

"I hope you're right," Bat muttered.

Dean Armanruder made the standard goodbyes and flicked the set off.

Bat said, "I got the impression that these fellows are tougher than President Fielding seems to think."

Armanruder flicked the set on again and said, "New

Woodstock, Mr. Blake, Mr. Stryn, Doctor Barnes, Mr. Terwilliger, Mr. Prager." He touched the control on the screen so that he could see all five faces at once.

When they appeared, he said, "Emergency meeting of the executive committee, gentlemen. Could you come at once to my home?"

When the executive committee had all assembled, Dean Armanruder had them seated in the salon. Jim Blake, the town's most successful artist, financially speaking, at least; Dag Stryn, also an artist and the guru of the town's New Temple movement; Doctor Barnes; Phil Terwilliger, who represented the retired element in New Woodstock, and Sam Prager, who more or less represented the mechanics and other workers in town. Miss Paskov, in all her full glory now, sat to one side, Bat to the other, of the retired corporation manager.

Dean Armanruder told the story himself, rather than Bat, but when it was over the questions were fired at the town's patrolman.

Sam Prager said, "How many were there, Bat?"

"I'm not sure. I saw only four. I heard the voices of at least three more. There might have been twenty, for all I know. Or more."

Old man Terwilliger said, his voice on the fearful side, "You think they were bluffing?"

Bat shook his head. "No. I could be wrong, but no."

"But why New Woodstock?" Dag Stryn said slowly. "The mobile towns that are really bothering them are the big ones that remain in one spot. I can see a certain amount of validity in their objecting to twenty thousand or so mobile houses parked in sites about, say, Acapulco. But New Woodstock is only some five hundred homes and on its way through, at that. It seems unlikely that we'll remain in Mexico for even a month."

79

Bat said, "They claimed that we were conspicuous because New Woodstock is an art colony composed of objectionable Bohemians, and they want to raise an international stink, a cause célèbre. However, I suspect there's another angle. We're small as towns go. We have, for instance, one full-time cop, one deputy, a couple of emergency assistant deputies. But if they were tangling with a town ten times or more our size, they'd run into considerably more trouble. Besides, we're off on the by-ways, on roads unpatrolled by the Mexican highway police. The big towns stick to the ultra-expressways where they wouldn't be vulnerable."

Terwilliger said, "I think we ought to go back."

"Certainly not," Jim Blake said heatedly. "What are we, a bunch of sissies? Bat is probably right. There's only five or six Mexican soreheads involved. Let's just call on the police."

"We already did," Bat said. "They didn't answer."

Blake said, "We'll call in the American authorities, then. We're all American citizens."

"I'm not," Sam Prager said. "I'm a Canadian, but the thing is, we're in Mexico and under the jurisdiction of the Mexican authorities even if this is a predominantly American mobile town."

"We can issue a complaint to the American Consulate or Embassy in Mexico City."

"If we ever get to Mexico City," Bat said lowly.

The elderly Phil Terwilliger said, "I vote to turn back, before it's too late. I'm retired and have only a few years of life left to me. I have no intention of having the period shortened by desperate men shooting at me. And I also have my wife to consider."

"I'll vote to go back too," Dag Stryn said. "I'll continue

if the rest of you so decide, but it seems these people do not want us and if so we shouldn't intrude on them."

Dean Armanruder said, "A very small number, perhaps, don't want us but for that matter quite a few Americans in our own country don't like the mobile towns and cities. We can't please everyone. I vote to go on."

"I vote to go on," Jim Blake said loudly.

"So do I," Sam Prager said.

Doctor Barnes said, "At this point, they have done nothing except issue their ultimatum to Bat, here. Until we have evidence that they are really as determined as they say, I also vote to go on."

"The vote is four to two," Dean Armanruder said. "We will proceed. I suggest that the whole matter be kept confined to us here, there is no use alarming the possibly more timid elements in New Woodstock."

"Wait a minute," Bat said. "This isn't a matter for the executive committee to decide alone. You can't expose everyone to a possible danger without their even knowing about it. This is a matter of convening the assembly of New Woodstock. If we vote on such trivial matters as whether or not to stop for lunch, we certainly should vote on something as important as this."

Dean Armanruder looked at him disgustedly. "Your opinion is not needed, Hardin. As town police officer you have a voice but not a vote in this executive committee."

Bat said evenly, "And this is not a town that subscribes to one dollar, one vote, Mr. Armanruder. The opinion of any adult in town is just as valid as yours. As town police officer I demand a convening of the assembly."

"Bat's right," Sam Prager said. "It isn't up to us to decide, we'll have to call the assembly."

Doc Barnes nodded. "Obviously. I'm afraid it's going to mean a splitting up of the town. But we can't take innocent people into possible gunfire or other danger without giving them the opportunity of debating and voting on it."

X

While Nadine Paskov and Dean Armanruder were going through the routine of summoning the assembly of all residents of New Woodstock over the age of eighteen, Bat Hardin strolled back toward his vehicle in the company of Dag Stryn.

He glanced over at the other from the side of his eyes. "You know, one of their beefs about Americans was your new religious movement, the New Temple."

"Oh? How is that?"

"One of them called it a no-religion and complained that the simpler people, here in Mexico, enviously noted that the affluent Americans were tending in your direction. The obvious implication is that if they supported the same religion perhaps they, too, would be wealthy."

The big Norwegian chuckled. "No-religion, eh? Well, in a way I suppose he was right. I see the New Temple as teaching a code somewhere between that of the old Unitarian-Universalists and the Quakers, but I have heard it said that it was the nearest thing to an Agnostic Church that had ever been organized." He chuckled again. "If you could say that the New Temple was organized. Actually it's the most chaotic organization going."

Bat said, "I'm not particularly interested in religion. In fact, I'm not even an atheist. But if your outfit is so permissive, why bother at all?"

Stryn nodded. "Man is an ethical animal, Bat. The only one. So far as we know, he has always sought the gods and down through the ages what began as the simplest of superstition evolved into high ethical standards. Take, for instance, the Jewish faith. The first books of the Bible were pretty grim; the laws and history of a barbarous, warlike people. By the time of the latter prophets however, the Hebrew religion had achieved the highest levels to that date. Jesus, you know, taught nothing that was not to be found in the works of those Jews who had immediately preceded him as religious teachers. And both Christianity and later Mohammedanism were based on Jewish foundations."

"And the New Temple?"

Stryn shook his head. "Judaism and then Christianity and Mohammedanism all came out of a nomadic desert society and out of a socio-economic system of thousands of years ago. In many respects they no longer fit the world as we find it today. So we of the New Temple try to find new answers for the new questions. We need an ethical code suited to the world as it is today, not to nomadic semi-barbarianism."

"Well, do you believe in God?"

Stryn squinted quizzically at him. "What is God? That is one of the questions we ask."

"And what is the answer you come up with?"

"The answer is, we don't know, but continue to ask. Do you remember reading of a political party called the Know-Nothings in the early history of the United States?"

"Yes, a little," Bat said.

"Well, the New Temple is in somewhat the same position. We openly say, we know nothing. And possibly it is beyond us to *ever* know anything about God, or the gods, if such exist. Perhaps such a being as a god is so much above us that we will never be able to comprehend him. Among other things, has it ever occurred to

84

you that if there is a God, he might not be benevolent in his relations to man—if he bothers to have any at all."

"How do you mean?" Bat said.

"Well, take chickens and their relationship to man. They can't comprehend the workings of man. Were they a bit more intelligent, they might think of us as gods. We provide them with a roost for the night where they can be safe from foxes or other animals. During the day we protect them from chicken hawks and such enemies, and always we provide them with food and water. But certainly man's relationship to the chicken is not a benevolent one. We do all those things in order to steal their eggs and ultimately kill them for our tables."

Bat had to laugh. He said, "Well, I don't see why you bother to exist as an organization."

Stryn thought about it. "Man seeks," he said finally. "We continue to strive for more understanding. Perhaps some day we will reach out into the stars; perhaps we will achieve the godhead ourselves. One of the fields in which we strive is that of ethics. If there is evolution in man's society, certainly there is in his ethics. Consider, once again, how far we have come from the teachings of Moses—and his teachings were notable for his time."

"Whether or not he wrote them, or even whether or not he ever existed," Bat said wryly.

"Yes, of course. Quite likely the books of Genesis were ghosted by teachers who came much later. However, whoever wrote them were advanced for their times."

Bat said suddenly, "Dag, what do you get out of it? You're what they call a guru. Why?"

The viking-like Norwegian chuckled once more. "Nothing beyond satisfaction. That is one of the few rigid canons of the New Temple, Bat. No New Temple officer, guru or simple follower, can profit in any manner from his position. In past religions, priests, ministers, preachers, rabbis, imams and fakirs found means to enrich themselves. A new religion might start off with deliberately poverty-stricken men of the caliber of Joshua of Nazareth and his apostles, but within a few generations their supposed followers might be among the richest men in the community. Not the New Temple. If I took payment for anything pertaining to the organization, I would not only immediately lose my title of guru, which is largely honorary at any rate, but would even be dismissed from the New Temple itself."

Bat thought that over. He said, "Well, there are some jobs that have to be paid. Say, for example, that a group of you got together and built a place in which to congregate. If I understand it, you all pitch in and pony up the required funds. But, all right, then you need a janitor to maintain it. Doesn't he get paid?"

Dag Stryn nodded. "Yes, sometimes, if volunteers aren't adequate. But in this case the janitor's first requirement is that he not be a follower of the New Temple. He can be a Catholic, or a Buddhist, or an atheist for that matter, but he can't be a follower of the New Temple and profit in any manner from his membership."

Bat said, "Well, I can see that would eliminate opportunists and hypocrites." They had reached the vicinity of his two vehicles and he waved a goodbye at the New Temple guru who continued on to his own mobile home.

Bat went over to Sam Prager's home repair shop and knocked at the door. Edith Prager opened it. She was an intense woman who impressed Bat Hardin as having a culture complex beyond that usually associated with even inhabitants of an art colony. He liked Sam Prager but invariably felt uncomfortable in the presence of his wife.

She wrote poetry, Doc Barnes had said. Bat had never seen any of it and he suspected that he didn't want to.

"Hello, Mr. Hardin," she said, standing in the door without inviting him in.

"Good morning," he said. "Is Sam back from the meeting as yet?"

"No, he isn't. What's this about an assembly?"

"It's being organized now. When Sam comes, will you let him know that the screen on my car phone is broken? I think it's just the screen but I don't know."

She said sharply, "It'll take the whole unit possibly. Who's to pay?"

Bat said, "It's my own car, Mrs. Prager, but was damaged while on duty for the town. I assume the cost of parts will come out of town finances but I'll take the bill immediately and charge it to the town later on. Tell Sam I'd appreciate having him put high priority on this. A police car simply can't operate without a TV phone."

"I'll tell him," she said, and closed the door.

She seemed a bit abrupt. Bat remembered Jeff Smith and wondered if there were others in New Woodstock who, inwardly at least, objected to him because of his racial heritage.

It had been quite a time since he had even thought about the subject. In a town such as New Woodstock, you didn't expect to run into characters who bothered with such nonsense as race, color or religious beliefs. He wondered vaguely if there were any Jews in New Woodsock; he had never thought of that before, either. Was Prager a Jewish name, or Zogbaum? Damned if he knew.

Back in his parents' day being black or even mulatto had its definite disadvantages but that had been a couple of generations ago. Today, under the Meritocracy, you found your level through your own abilities and the man that sat at the desk next to you might just as soon be a Black or an Oriental as not. The fact that the old-time stastistics indicated that the Black race was less educable and less intelligent than the White were proving less and less valid.

He reentered his mobile house and took up a folding chair and, carrying it, went back to the center of the site.

Others were already setting up their own chairs in a large horseshoe-like semicircle.

It came to him that this was a present-day equivalent of the old Town Meeting of New England, or, possibly, something like the governing of the Swiss Confederation of cantons. It was a working democracy in which every adult had his say because the governing unit was small enough so that power and responsibility didn't have to be delegated.

By and large, it worked. It wasn't the only method utilized to govern mobile cities and towns, of course. New Woodstock was small enough to put it over but the really large cities had city payrolls and full-time officials. However, some of the towns, usually ones that were even smaller than New Woodstock, sometimes had governments ranging from pseudo-communism to out-and-out anarchy—in short, no government at all. Bat had to smile inwardly when he realized that the other mobile town he had lived with, the one composed largely of archeology buffs, had in actuality been one of the anarchy types. It had been a madhouse when some decision had to be made.

The executive committee and Nadine Paskov, who had a portable TV phone before her, sat behind a table facing the assembly of town adults. Bat took his chair and sat it to one end of the table in view of the fact that undoubtedly he'd be called on frequently.

When all except a few straggling latecomers had found places, Dean Armanruder opened the meeting by pounding with the gavel of the executive committee's senior member.

He came immediately to the point. "Mr. Hardin has requested a convening of the assembly on the grounds that the community has been threatened with physical danger and must decide whether or not to continue this move to South America. Mr. Hardin."

Bat was moderately surprised. He had expected the retired corporation manager to sum up the situation. In actuality, Bat Hardin had had little experience in public speaking and was a victim of both stage fright and inarticulateness. However, he did as well as he could and sat down as quickly as he could, feeling a little ashamed of himself. In his time he had charged full into automatic weapon fire with less quailing than this.

When he had finished, stunned silence met his words for a moment.

Dean Armanruder cleared his throat. "The question before us, citizens of New Woodstock, is whether to proceed, or whether to return to the United States. The floor is open to discussion."

For a long moment, no one requested permission to speak.

Finally, "The chair recognizes Mr. Jeff Smith."

Smith stood next to his folding seat and looked about him deliberately. "I think the first thing to consider is whether this whole story is a lot of crap."

XI

There was another moment of shocked silence and then a muttering, then a jabbering, only part of it in indignation.

Dean Armanruder rapped them to silence.

He looked at Jeff Smith, still standing, a defiant smirk on his face. The senior executive committee member said evenly, "Mr. Smith, you have either said too much or too little. Please elucidate."

Jeff Smith rapped, "For the first part of this story we have only the word of Hardin and Zogbaum, from whom we haven't as yet heard, but I assume he'll back his fellow barroom brawler. They say they went into town and the Mexicans started a fight. That's what they say. Evidently, the Linares chief of police sees it otherwise."

"You're damn right I back Bat Hardin," Ferd Zogbaum called.

Dean Armanruder rapped with his gavel. "That will be all at this time, Mr. Zogbaum. We follow Robert's Rules of Order here. Continue, Mr. Smith."

Jeff Smith went on. "The second part of the story has nothing to back it whatsoever and on its face is a pretty fanciful tale. Mexico is a civilized country. Armed vigilantes don't attack peaceful tourists. What Hardin's purpose is, I wouldn't know. For some reason he evidently doesn't want to see New Woodstock continue to our destination, South America. He wants to turn back. Possibly he's afraid of the long trip ahead and

90

would rather remain in the States where life is admittedly easier, especially for the town's peace officer."

The assembly buzzed again and Armanruder rapped for silence.

He looked at Bat Hardin and said, "Do you have anything to say to this, Mr. Hardin?"

"No," Bat said.

Armanruder looked back at Jeff Smith. "And what is your proposal, Mr. Smith?"

"I propose, first, that we go on, as planned. And secondly that we depose this alarmist and elect a new police officer."

Armanruder said, "It is not the most desirable among the town's volunteer positions, Mr. Smith. Whom would you suggest as an alternative to Mr. Hardin?"

"Anyone. His now deputy, Al Castro, could certainly do better."

Al Castro called, "No thanks. Bat's the man, so far as I'm concerned. I'm happy to stay on as his deputy but I wouldn't take his job as long as he wants it."

Armanruder rapped with his gavel. "Please ask for recognition by the chair before stating your opinions, Mr. Castro."

But Al added, his voice loud and clear, "I've never heard Bat Hardin tell a lie as long as I've known him."

Armanruder gave another double rap. "Go on, Mr. Smith."

Smith said, "If no one else will volunteer for the job, I make the following motion. That Hardin be dismissed and that I be made town police officer."

There was silence for a moment.

Finally, Jim Blake said, 'For the sake of bringing it to the vote, I'll second that motion. And I'll also vote for Bat Hardin being retained."

Armanruder said, "Motion has been moved and seconded. Bat Hardin to be replaced by Jeff Smith as police officer of New Woodstock. Miss Paskov, you are tied into the computer for voting?"

"Yes, sir."

Dean Armanruder looked at the assembly. "To simplify, if there is no objection, cast your vote for either Mr. Smith or Mr. Hardin."

There was little hesitation. Each member of the assembly put his or her pocket phone to mouth and cast the vote.

"Have all voted?" Armanruder said.

No one spoke up.

He said, "Miss Paskov?"

Nadine Paskov said dryly, "There were two votes for Mr. Smith."

A laugh tittered through the assembly.

Jeff Smith flushed angrily and sat down.

Bat Hardin, obviously, was gratified. However, he knew that there were various persons in the town who weren't particularly friendly toward him. He wondered if his victory was a matter of the lesser of two evils. Though they might not think him the best of all possible cops, they were pretty sure that Jeff Smith would be a damned sight worse. He also wondered vaguely who had cast the second vote for Smith, who had obviously voted for himself.

Armanruder was saying, "We have all, except two, evidently accepted the truthfulness of Mr. Hardin's story, that he was kidnapped and the town threatened. How large an element has threatened us, we cannot say, but a threat has been made. Further comments before we put to a vote whether or not we should retreat?"

Ferd Zogbaum raised his hand and was recognized.

He stood and said, an indignation in his tone, "When we decided to make this trek, all the way to South America, did any of us labor under the illusion that it was all going to be peaches and cream? Didn't we realize that we proposed to go through some of the wildest country remaining in North, Central and South America? Didn't we realize that there was going to be all sorts of hardship and accident before we got through? Didn't we all accept that some of our vehicles would break down, that some of us, before we were through, would possibly die from one cause or the other? Didn't we all know that there would be bad weather, landslides earthquakes, and possibly bandits? Very well. This is our first stop. Is it going to be our last south of the border? Are we going to chicken out at the first threat—not actuality, thus far, just a threat—of danger?"

He sat down abruptly.

Armanruder said, "Thank you Mr. Zogbaum. Anyone else?"

Phil Terwilliger requested permission to speak.

He said, "It is all very well for a young man such as Mr. Zogbaum to be so gung ho, to wish to press on into adventure. However, when my wife, who is already quite ill, and I voted to take this trip with the rest of the town, we did not expect to be bitten by snakes in Nicaragua, or buried by a landslide in Costa Rica, nor . . ." his elderly voice went sarcastic ". . . attacked by headhunting Indians in Ecuador. We had been of the opinion that with the advent of the Pan American Highway it was quite possible these days to travel all the way to our destination in reasonable comfort and safety. However, if on our first day we are threatened by a body of armed men, one of whom told Mr. Hardin that he wouldn't particularly mind shooting him, then I think we have stuck our necks into something more than we had originally planned. I strongly urge that we turn back as a town. But if you others vote to go on then I, at least, will disassociate myself from New Woodstock and return to the States to take up residence in some other mobile town or city."

There were others. They spoke in varying degrees of heat, indignation or fearfulness, some taking one side, some the other.

When it was finally put to the vote, four-fifths of the assembly were for going on. The remainder refused to accept the decision of the majority and decided to return in a body to Texas. The returnees numbered approximately one hundred of the mobile homes, largely those owned by the more elderly.

The question then became what to do with the community property such as the auxiliary vehicles and the town treasury, which was not overly large. The treasury was accumulated by a slight tax on all citizens of the town, or a community assessment if an emergency of more than usual magnitude developed.

Since the vote had gone so strongly for the element that wished to go on, it was decided that all auxiliaries remain with New Woodstock and that those that were returning be recompensed out of town funds for their share of what they left behind.

And the question then became, where were these funds to come from, since the treasury held no such amount?

This was solved by several of the more affluent town members such as Armanruder, Doctor Barnes and Jim Blake making a loan to the town which would be repaid as rapidly as tax money came in. A small levy was also to be made, small enough as not to be a strain even on citizens who existed solely on their NIT, to help in the transaction.

Still another problem arose. Among those who were to return was the middle-aged Barbara Stevens, the competent nurse of Doctor Barnes. He had two or three other practical nurses in the town, or whom he could call in emergency, but Miss Stevens was the only professional.

It was decided immediately to issue a call through the United Mobile Cities Association and its TV newspaper for a nurse, preferably a volunteer, but, if necessary, one who could be put on the town payroll.

Someone suggested that very possibly they could pick up a nurse in Mexico City who would work for considerably less pay than an American, if no American on NIT volunteered to take the position without recompense.

Someone else suggested that the Mexican nurse, if one was found, be offered free living quarters in the hospital. This would lessen the amount of pay necessary and New Woodstock was too small a town to support much in the way of a town payroll. It was also pointed out that a Mexican nurse would be a double advantage. She would be able to communicate in Spanish all the way down to South America, in Spanish medical terms. Doctor Barnes did not have Spanish, and there were very few in the whole town who did.

XII

In all, the meeting of the assembly took several hours and Bat Hardin could see that they wouldn't be getting away that day. He didn't like it. He didn't like giving the vigilantes under Don Caesar the extra time to consolidate their forces and to prepare for whatever trouble they had in mind against New Woodstock.

But there was nothing for it. Even after the assembly had adjourned, there was considerable to be done in the breakaway of the hundred mobile homes that had decided to return to the States. And when all business had been handled, there was still the personal relationships that had in some instances been abuilding for years. Artists, of whatever sort, have a tendency toward emotionalism, and many a tear was shed, many a kiss exchanged. In fact, many a drink was knocked back after an appropriate toast. Bat had a sneaking suspicion that the hundred defectors wouldn't return in a body to McAllen, Texas, but would straggle back.

In the old days, folk who lived in what were then trailers, moved about as individuals. It wasn't until after the Second World War that the first beginnings of the mobile towns and cities began to manifest themselves. They started, possibly, as the trailer clubs, groups of compatible persons who would get together during vacations and take a tour, in company, to here, there, or the other place, usually to some National Park or other attraction. At that same time, the large trailer sites were

96

developing where people lived in supposedly mobile homes but who, in actuality, never moved or, at least, seldom did. Indeed, many of the so-called mobile homes of that day were incapable of being moved, their wheels long since gone, or, at least, their tires flat and their axles rusting away.

The permanent mobile home parks still remained, developed considerably, with enlarged facilities and with governmental systems. And these were largely populated with the more elderly and sedentary types. They were to be found in all parts of the country, in fact in all parts of North America, but largely in the climatic and scenically desirable areas. They were strung out along the West Coast from Washington to Baja California, strung out along both Floridian coasts and far up into Georgia and the Carolinas and along the Gulf coast to Brownsville, Texas, and beyond. The high altitudes of Arizona and New Mexico were dotted everywhere with them and up into Colorado and Utah and, in the United States proper, as far north as Glacier National Park.

But it was the mobile town which actually kept on the move that was really the innovation of the new post-industrial state. Where in the past the trailer clubs had taken to the road for a few weeks at a time during the vacation periods, now, with the coming of NIT, large elements of the population were on what amounted to permanent vacation. And those with itchy feet kept on all but constant move. Oh, they might stop and pause, here or there, whenever the attraction was such that a prolonged stay seemed desirable, but largely they kept on the move. And while they had begun with, at most, a few dozen campers, trailers and mobile homes, the numbers increased and eventually what had been trailer clubs became mobile villages, then towns, then cities.

And by the looks of things the end was not yet in sight. Certainly, a city of fifty thousand was no longer maximum. Each year that went by they became larger until sometimes Bat Hardin wondered if the whole nation would take to wheels.

But that of course was ridiculous. The high rise pseudo-cities were also on the increase, inhabited by people who desired urban life of the old type. Persons who wanted the theatres, the restaurants and nightclubs, the museums, the more extensive shopping facilities that mobile towns could never enjoy. Not all Americans by any means had the travel itch. Many a present-day American had descended from ancestors who had come from the ancient, crowded medieval cities, not to speak of the ghettos, of Europe and, under pressure, came to the New World only to immediately duplicate their former environment.

Bat headed in the direction of Sam Prager's home and repair shop.

Sam was seated, sprawled rather, before his vehicles, in the same folding chair he had occupied at the assembly shortly before. He was scowling in thought.

Bat said, "Having second thoughts about going on?"

The other stirred. "No, not really. But I must say, I didn't expect to run into a hassle such as this, so soon, anyway."

"Nor did I," Bat admitted. "I didn't know you were a Canadian, Sam."

"No particular reason to mention the fact. There's precious little difference between a Canadian such as myself and a Yankee such as you, these days."

Bat had to laugh. "Calling me a Yankee is on the side of stretching a point. I'm getting called just about everything today, starting with gringo this morning. But I'm somewhat surprised that you're not with one of the Canadian mobile towns."

Sam shrugged. "Easier to find work in a Yank town. No competition. Not many of you have to work. You have NIT. We haven't come to that, as yet at least, in Canada. Knock on wood."

Bat looked at him questioningly. "You don't approve of NIT?"

"Nope. Makes bums of people. Man was created to make his bread by the sweat of his brow."

Actually, Bat Hardin largely agreed with him, but he said, "The thing is, man doesn't eat bread much, any more. We're calorie conscious."

Sam snorted at him. "You know what I mean."

"Yes, and I read an interesting discussion on it the other day. The idea was that man has taken his full career to get to the point where he can produce an abundance with a minimum of labor. It took the whole human race a million years and more to get here. Along the line, hundreds of thousands, millions of our ancestors contributed. Fire was discovered by some, agriculture by others, domestication of animals by others, ceramics, the use of metals, the first simple sciences by still others. Over the centuries, this ancestor and that added his contribution, great or small, to man's accumulating knowledge. Finally, we've arrived at the point where we have abundance. A man who works today, sitting before some unbelievably complicated automatic machinery, supposedly producing hundreds of thousands of units of this commodity or that, isn't actually producing all that product himself. It is the human race, back through the centuries, that is producing it. And thus the product is the common heritage of us all. If we have gotten to the point where all of us need not work, are unneeded, it is not the fault of the individual that he doesn't participate in our agriculture or industry. But still, at least a basic living is his heritage."

Sam took him in sceptically. "It's a great theory. Do you believe it?"

Bat said, grinning sourly, "Well, no. Actually, I think you're right. A man should work. Which brings us to the point. Did you finish repairing my phone screen?"

Sam stood up and turned toward the door of his combined home and shop. "Yeah. I had to put in an entire new unit, Bat. You going to pay for it, or should I bill the town?"

"Just to speed things up, I'll pay you. I'll take the bill to Armanruder later. He's too busy now. I know you work on a limited budget and can probably use the credit right away."

"That I can. Come on in, Bat."

Bat Hardin followed the electronic repairman into his shop. Edith Prager didn't seem to be around; probably up in the living quarters, Bat decided, getting ready to leave.

Sam Prager had a licensed credit exchanger attached to his TV phone screen as a result of his trade. Bat Hardin put his pocket phone, credit card on the screen and his thumbprint on the square at the screen's side and looked at Sam.

Sam said, "Twenty-three pseudo-dollars and fifty cents."

Bat said into the screen, "Please credit to Sam Prager twenty-three pseudo-dollars and fifty cents from my balance."

The screen said, "Transaction completed."

Bat took up his phone and returned it to his pocket. He said to Sam, "Do you have a gun?"

Sam said, "Yes. A carbine. I thought we'd possibly be

running into deer, wild pig and that sort of thing down in Central and South America."

"Does Edith drive?"

"Sure."

"I suggest that when we take off, you let her drive and you sit next to her with the carbine."

Sam hissed a low whistle. "You really expect trouble, don't you, Bat?"

Bat didn't want to overly alarm the town. He said, "Not necessarily, but there's no harm in being ready. If anybody does take a shot at us, I'd like to see an immediate response big enough to set them back on their heels. If you had to take the time to stop your car and hustle back into the interior of your home to find your gun, then load it, then dash to some point where you could return the fire, the whole thing might be over before you got into the action. If you're sitting up there in front, gun on lap, you'll blast back at him before the echo of his own shot has faded."

"Makes sense," Sam nodded.

"See you, Sam."

"So long, Bat."

Bat started in the direction of Dean Armanruder's home, thinking about it. The instructions he had just given Sam Prager had come to him on the spur of the moment but the more he considered it, the more he liked the idea.

Armanruder was standing before his mobile mansion talking to Doc Barnes. Bat came up and stood off a few yards until the two older men became aware of his presence.

Barnes said, "Bat?"

Bat came forward and said, "I think it might be a good idea if you'd give me carte blanche on organizing the line of march tomorrow."

"How's that, Hardin?" the former magnate said.

"Well, I've got a double motive. First, I think common sense dictates that we take off from Linares as ready for trouble as we can be, even though it doesn't materialize. We want no stragglers, for one thing. I'm of the opinion that if a mobile home breaks down between here and the Pan American Highway, which should be safe, it should be abandoned and its inhabitants taken up to go on with us."

Doc Barnes said slowly, "I doubt if many of our people would simply leave their homes right next to the highway, Bat."

Bat fixed his eyes on him. "Doc, I feel so strongly that nobody should be left behind that I suggest that if it becomes necessary to abandon one of our homes, or even more, that the owners be recompensed out of the New Woodstock town funds."

Dean Armanruder puffed up his cheeks. "That becomes quite a drain on the treasury, Hardin. And it's already bare as a result of having to pay off the hundred homes that are turning back for their share of the community property."

Bat said doggedly, "Under the circumstances, we can't let anyone fall behind. Probably, we'll all get through to the Pan American Highway. But a breakdown can always happen and I'm certainly not in favor of all of us stopping and remaining indefinitely until repairs are completed. Our best chance is to push on as fast as possible. If we stopped, up there in the hills, we'd be sitting ducks for any snipers, or whatever."

"Ummm," Armanruder said, "And you say you had a double motive?"

"Sir, usually when a mobile town moves, it proceeds more or less haphazardly. When you start off in the morning, everybody knows the destination. So some start early, some take off in small groups, some lag behind. Sometimes, units lag behind for days. All right. I think that tomorrow New Woodstock should be a veritable hedgehog. Women driving, those men who possess guns sitting next to them, ready for action. I think we should drive almost bumper-to-bumper, looking for any trouble, and ready for it if it materializes."

Doc Barnes muttered, "Sounds like a confounded military convoy."

Bat said softly, "It is."

Dean Armanruder was thinking about it, unhappily.

Bat said, "I'd like to put this on the community phone. You see, I suspect we have a leak. Ordinarily, our community phone wouldn't be tapped by outsiders. But I suspect that anything that goes over it is forwarded to Don Caesar, or whoever. If so, then they'll pick up this move of ours and perhaps our very readiness will dissuade them."

Armanruder was taken aback. "A leak? What in the world do you mean by that?"

"I mean that Don Caesar's men were tipped off that I was coming up that road this morning. On top of that, my pocket phone was taken from me by the kidnappers but was sitting on my table when I returned. I suspect that they were trying to throw a scare into me, showing how efficient they were. And I doubt if a complete stranger to New Woodstock could have done it. He wouldn't have known where my home was parked and he would have been spotted wandering through the town, even if he did know."

"That sounds fantastic," Doc Barnes said.

Bat looked in his direction. "Got any other explanation, Doc?"

103

"Why, no."

Armanruder said, "All right, all right. You're the police officer. So far as I'm concerned, you can make any arrangement you wish pertaining to our so-called order of march tomorrow. Go into my office, if you wish, and use the desk phone there. You'll be more comfortable."

Bat nodded and said, "One other thing. I suggest we make all preliminary arrangements for leaving tonight and that we roll at first flush of dawn. These people confronting us—if they're confronting us—are not professional military. I doubt if they're very well organized. Civilians lack discipline. We might catch them unawares and be completely through the mountains while they're still comfortably in their beds."

"That sounds reasonable," Armanruder admitted. "Notify the town to that effect, Hardin."

But Bat shook his head. "No. That wouldn't do. We'll have to pass that on by word of mouth, not put it on the air. That might tip them off, if they have some way of tapping our communications."

"How about this leak of yours?" Doctor Barnes demanded. "If there is such a traitor among us, he'll let them know."

Bat nodded again. "Of course. And, if so, then we'll know we've got a traitor and not just suspect it."

"You handle it, Hardin," Armanruder said.

"Thank you, sir," Bat said. "I'll put the assistant deputies to going from home to home explaining the situation."

He went over to the major entrance of the Armanruder home and found the door open. He entered and headed for the office. He had noted that Dean Armanruder hadn't bothered to put the matter to a vote with the executive committee, but had arbitrarily made the decision himself. Bat hadn't liked that, but on the other hand he didn't want to take the chance that the executive committee might overrule the idea. They weren't men of action; he doubted if any of them had ever been in combat.

Nadine Paskov, in mini-shorts and sandals, and nothing else, and certainly no advertisement for expansion of the textile industry, met him in the hall.

"What are you doing here?" she demanded, but making no move to shield her almost complete nudity.

Bat said, "Mr. Armanruder suggested that I use his office phone to issue a general plan for tomorrow's move."

"Tomorrow? Aren't we leaving today? The sooner we get out of here the better I'll like it."

He shook his head. "It would seem safer if we left so early in the morning that most Mexicans would be in bed. In Mexico, mornings are chilly. No Mexican in his right mind arises before the sun is really up there."

Suddenly, she put a hand on his arm. "Bat, is there really danger? I thought this was all a lot of nonsense."

He said carefully, "There probably isn't but the safe thing is to go ahead as though there is. The better prepared we are, the less danger there is."

"Do you think these people might really shoot at us?"

Oh, oh.

Bat said carefully, "They might, but I'm not really expecting it. We just want to tread carefully, Miss Paskov."

"Look, Bat, perhaps I should go back with the others to Texas."

He cocked his head slightly to one side, gnawing his underlip. "Why don't you?"

She took a breath. "It's the best job I could ever get."

"You could always go on NIT, if you couldn't get another."

"NIT, NIT! Poverty level, subsistence level income!"

"Well, it's not as bad as all that. What they call poverty level nowadays would have been considered wealth a hundred years ago."

"We're not living a hundred years ago, we're living now. Do you know what these clothes I'm wearing cost?"

He almost laughed at that, but held it in. She could have bought the shorts and sandals she wore in one of the swank snob shops in some northern city, and he had no idea what she might have had to pay for them, but excellent copies were available, certainly, in any ultramarket back in the States and probably right here in Mexico.

He said, "It's your decision, Miss Paskov. You can go back with the others, or on with us."

She said, urgently, "But you don't understand. He's written me into his will. I can't quit."

Bat was beginning to get impatient with her, aware of the need for him to go about his business. He said, "I don't see how I can help you in your decision."

She said, "Look. This mobile monstrosity will attract the most attention. It's so big. If anybody shoots at our town, they'll shoot at it first."

"Well, not necessarily. . . ."

She stepped closer to him, breathing deeply so that the pointed tips of her breasts jiggled. She said, "Yes, yes they will and everything is plastic. A bullet would go right through. Look, Bat, your car is armored, isn't it?"

"Yes." He looked at her in sudden realization of what she was building up to.

She said urgently, looking him full in the eyes. "Bat,

106

if you let me ride with you tomorrow, when we make camp tomorrow night, I'll come to your trailer. I'll . . . I'll let you do anything you want to me. Anything. Or, if you'd rather have something special I'll do anything to you you want, Bat. Anything at all."

Bat shook his head and said wearily, "Tomorrow I'll be riding out in front. If they've got something up their sleeves such as mining the road with dynamite, or dropping a neat little avalanche off some mountain peak, I'll get it first. See here, Miss Paskov, if you're afraid, I'd certainly give it a long thinking over before continuing all the way to South America. It's like Ferd Zogbaum said at the assembly, we're most likely going to run into bigger emergencies than this before we arrive."

"But I'm in the old fool's *will*."

Bat couldn't think of anything to say to that. He side-stepped her and continued on to the office. Christ, but she was a handsome woman. He snorted inwardly. He wouldn't touch her with a long, long pole indeed.

He sat down at Armanruder's desk, activated the TV phone and said into the screen, "New Woodstock, General Call."

And then, "Please hear this. This is Bat Hardin, your town police officer. With the concurrence of Mr. Armanruder, I strongly make the following suggestions. That all of us who are armed, ride with our weapons in hand. Women should drive, when possible. If fired upon en route, return as heavy a barrage as possible. Even if you do not see an immediate target, fire in the direction from which the attack came. I want as large a display of firepower as we can muster. Even if you have a weapon of no larger caliber than a twenty-two, have it in hand. If you have only a shotgun, load it with as heavy a load as you have, either slugs or buckshot would be best. If you do not have

107

a weapon, try to borrow one from those among us who have more than one.

"We shall proceed with several of our younger single men in the lead vehicles. If we run into a roadblock, it shall be their duty to clear it, even under fire. We'll want volunteers for the lead vehicles. Please contact me. When we move, it will be bumper to bumper and no stragglers will be allowed. In case of breakdown, the mobile home involved must be abandoned and its occupants taken in by its neighbors. We'll send mechanics back for it from the next Mexican city which has suitable garages. If the house is destroyed, the owner will later be recompensed from the town treasury. If there are any questions, please consult with either me or Mr. Armanruder."

He paused for a moment, and could think of nothing else. He finished with, "For the time, that is all," and flicked off the set.

He sat there for a moment, thinking out further plans, then came to his feet and left. He didn't see Nadine Paskov on his way out, which was all right with him. She was possibly embarrassed after having promised to put out for him if he'd let her ride in his car, and then having him turn her down. He hated to have someone as nervous as she in the convoy. Fear is contagious. They needed to keep their cool, especially if they actually did run into grief.

He walked over to Al Castro's house and found his deputy talking to Luke Robertson, standing in front of Al's mobile home. They cut short their conversation at his approach. He gave them a quick rundown on his plans and they nodded agreement.

Bat said to Al Castro, "I'm going to let you take my usual place in the column. I'll precede the town by about two kilometers. We'll be tuned into each other all the time. You do the same as everyone else, that is, let Pamela drive and you have your Gyro-jet pistol ready in your hand. Keep in continual touch with both me and Luke, here. Luke, you bring up the rear. Have young Tom Benton riding with you. My phone and Al's will be continually open to you; we'll be on a three-way hookup."

They were both nodding.

He bit his heavy lower lip and hesitated before adding, "Boys, once we're under way, ignore anything from Mr. Armanruder or anybody else on the executive committee, until we get to the Pan American Highway. Once we're underway, we're in command."

Al said, his voice slightly hesitant, "Have you checked this out with Armanruder?"

"No."

Luke Robertson said, "And don't. But we're not in command, Bat, you are."

"Yeah," Al said.

"Okay," Bat said. "There is no democracy when you're in combat. If anything happens to me, you take over, Al."

He gave them the information about their leaving at first dawn and told them to spread the word. They took off immediately on the task.

Bat turned and headed for the camper of Ferd Zogbaum. However, on the way he passed the mobile home of Diana Sward, and found Ferd there idly talking with the feminine artist who was cleaning paint brushes.

They gave him the standard friendly greeting and he explained the plans for the following morning to them.

Di said, "Look, if you can round up some kid or woman who can drive my electro-steamer, I'll help ride shotgun on this convoy, Bat. I've got a deer rifle."

"You can shoot?"

"Friend," she said. "I told you I was the daughter of a Grafin. A German aristocrat is trained to ride and shoot as well as balance a teacup, the pinky correctly arched. I'll lay you two to one I can zero-in on a bull's eye just as well as you can, military training or not."

"No bet," Bat said. "I'll take your word for it. I suggest that when we take off in the morning you station yourself behind some home such as Jim Blake's. I have a sneaking suspicion that even if Jim has a gun he couldn't hit the side of a barn from inside."

Bat turned to Ferd and said, "Ferd, you're cool when the bets are all down. I'd like you to take second place in the column behind Al Castro. If they hit us———"

Ferd said, "I don't have a gun, Bat."

"Oh." Bat Hardin rubbed the side of his face. "Well, there are a lot of homes in New Woodstock with more than one. Some of our people are hunting buffs. Seek one out and———"

Ferd Zogbaum, looking into his face, said, "I can't carry a gun, Bat."

Bat scowled lack of understanding. He had seen Ferd Zogbaum in action the night before and couldn't have done better in the clutch himself.

"How do you mean?"

Ferd Zogbaum's lips were white. "I'm not allowed to carry a gun."

Bat looked at him in amazement.

Ferd said, "I'm a felon, Bat."

XIII

"A what?" Diana Sward blurted.

He looked at her emptily. "I'm a paroled convict, Diana."

The three of them held a long silence.

Finally, Bat said, uncomfortably, "Well, nevertheless, this is an emergency. There are women and children involved. You're a good man. We need you."

Ferd sucked in air and made a face. "You don't understand. I *can't* carry a gun. You see, I've got a bug planted in my skull."

That made no sense to either Di or Bat.

Ferd said doggedly, "I mean an electronic bug. Everything I say is monitored. If I have a gun, or if I get into violence, I get a splitting headache and have to report immediately to my parole officer—by TV phone, of course."

"Holy smokes," Bat said in protest.

"It's better than being in a prison cell, Bat. There have been recent changes in penology that a lot of people don't know about. Today, most convicted . . . criminals aren't kept in prison. Even lifers, such as myself."

"Life?" Di said.

"Yes, I'm a three-time loser, Di. For the rest of my life I'll carry this bug. If I have a gun in my possession, or if I participate in violence, my head aches unbearably until I report. They have a continual fix on me, always know exactly where I am. They don't even care if

I leave the country. If they wanted, they could drop me in my tracks, any place in the world. But at least I can carry on a reasonably normal life. It's not like the old days, when you had to spend your time in a jail cell. Of course, if I wish to do certain things, take a job, or get married, for instance, I have to report in. Then my parole officer decides if I can do it or not. A woman is warned that I am a felon, a boss is also so informed." He added wryly, "Few woman wish to marry a felon, and few bosses want one to work for him. However, we're eligible for NIT."

Bat said, uncomfortably, "What are you . . . well, what were you sentenced for, Ferd?"

Ferd, his lips white again, said, "Are you asking me as a police officer?"

"Don't be an ass," Di said.

Bat said, "Of course not, primarily as a friend."

"You have to ask me as a police officer, so I can explain later to my parole officer."

"What in the hell are you talking about?"

Ferd sucked in air. This was hard for him. "Everything I say is monitored. If I use certain words, the computers report it to my parole office and I have to have an explanation."

Bat Hardin shook his head in disbelief but said, "All right, I ask you as a police officer."

Ferd said, as though apologetically, "It's like I told you, I'm under twenty-four-hour a day monitoring of everything I say. If I use terms like guns, robbery, fight, revolution, oh, scores of different terms that apply to crime of any sort, then my parole officer is notified and the complete conversation is then played back to him. And I have to explain. If I can't explain, too often, then it's either more brain surgery or back to prison for me."

"All right," Bat said. "As town police officer, I ask, what were you given life for, Ferd?"

"Conspiracy to commit subversive acts against the government."

They both ogled him.

He shrugged. "You asked me. I told you. Shortly, I'll get my headache and have to report to my parole officer. They caught me three times. I was easy to catch. Anybody's easy to catch these days when you can't exist without a credit card and when the computer data banks know everything about you that there is to know."

Diana Sward was looking at him strangely. "At least all this helps my ego. I've been wondering why, no matter how provocative I try to be, you haven't made the slightest effort to get into my pants. I thought my girlish charms must be fading."

He looked at her emptily. "Don't think I'm not susceptible. But how would you like to have a lover, every word of which he said was being listened to by a computer, or a parole officer, or two? Can you imagine these characters sitting around, some afternoon when things are slack, playing back some of the conversations that are put on the magnetic tapes? A love scene? The things a man says to a woman in bed?"

He clasped his hands suddenly to his head. "I shouldn't have said that," he muttered in agony. "I'll have to go."

They stared after him as he stumbled away.

"Good grief," Di blurted.

Bat said, "I'd think it'd almost be better to be in a cell."

"Oh, Bat," she said. "The poor sonofabitch."

Bat said in disgust, "Subversion! In this day and age? What possible chance could there be of overthrowing the government when every slob in the country is getting a free ride with his NIT? Not one person in twenty is dissatisfied with Meritocracy."

She viewed him from the side of her eyes. "I wonder."

As usual in the privacy of the camp ground, Diana Sward was both barefooted and topless. Her clothing bill must have been truly minimal; she seldom wore more than a pair of men's denim pants, cut short. Now, she knocked at the door of the camper before her.

It opened and a wan Ferd Zogbaum said, "Oh, hi Diana. Come on in." He stepped back to allow her entry.

She looked about the small, neat interior and shook her head. "All you bachelors are the same. Neat as goddamned pins. Bat's trailer is disgusting; it's so much cleaner than mine."

"Partly military training," Ferd said. "They teach you to be neat in the military, or you get the works. Sit down, Di. Could I get you a drink?"

She said, still standing, hipshot, "In a minute. Did you make your report?"

He took her in, almost as though suspiciously, "Well, yes, I did."

"No more headache?"

"No," he told her. "No more headache. The report was accepted. I was able to use the words that they monitor me on since I was talking to a police officer."

"Listen," she said deliberately. "When they monitor your conversations, do they hear what the other person says as well? What I mean is, are they picking up what I'm saying now?"

"No, of course not. Only what I say. They only hear one half of the conversation."

"All right. If you say nothing more than yes and no, then they don't give a damn?"

"Of course not. At first it's difficult, but after a while you learn to avoid saying words that are taboo."

"Okay."

"Okay what?"

She stepped closer to him and put her arms around his neck and pressed her fabulous breasts against his chest. "Don't say anything except yes or no to me. And how do you get the bed out in this camper?"

XIV

In the very first flush of dawn, Bat Hardin took off in his police car. He wasn't pulling his mobile home. He had left it for Ferd Zogbaum to draw behind his camper. It would slow Ferd down but he'd be able to manage.

Bat and his deputies had been lining the town up for the past two hours and it was as ready to roll as it would ever be. There had been a great buzz of excitement but for some reason everybody had tended to speak in whispers.

He had both Al Castro and Luke Robertson on his car phone; the screen split so that both of their faces could be there at once.

He passed Linares. The town was dead at this hour of the morning. When he was two kilometers along the road he looked at Al Castro and said, "Okay, Al, let the town roll."

Al Castro yawned mightily and murmured, "Here we come."

They had agreed to attempt to keep at a one hundred kilometer an hour clip, if possible, and Bat Hardin remained at that speed. Light was coming on fast now and his head was continually in motion, peering to the right of the road, to the left, continually checking his rear vision mirrors.

He kept in continual communication with Al Castro and Luke Robertson, checking their speeds. Everything was going fine. All during the night, the town's mechanics had worked on the engines of any electro-steamers that were suspect of possible breakdown. Thus far, all was tight, no stragglers.

At almost the exact spot where he had been halted the morning before, he came to a sudden halt. Leaning nonchalantly against a lone mesquite tree by the side of the road was the one they had called José. He seemed to be alone, nor was there any cover in the immediate vicinity which might have held others.

Bat said into the phone screen, "Al."

"Yeah."

"Slow down to about twenty-five. One of the clowns who picked me up yesterday is here."

"Okay."

His Gyro-jet carbine, which fired the exact same 9mm rocket shell as the pistol which had been appropriated yesterday, was on the seat beside him but he left it there. The other had no weapon—in hand, at least.

Bat got out of the car and approached. José stood erect and looked at him scornfully.

"So, gringo, you didn't bother to listen to our warning."

Bat said, "Some did. About a hundred of our mobile homes turned back to return to Texas."

"It isn't enough," the other told him. "This is your last warning, gringo. Turn back now and return to the States or what will happen is your own fault."

Bat shook his head. "We've made our decision. We have permission of the Mexican authorities to enter and travel through Mexico." He added, "As you know, there are women and children and elderly people in this town."

"We did not ask them to come to our country," the other said flatly. "They too contribute to the corruption that you gringos bring wherever you go."

Bat Hardin, in a quick flow of motion, stepped closer and drove his left fist into the other's stomach. José, his eyes popping in agony, folded forward and Bat slugged him brutally in the jaw. The Mexican collapsed onto the ground. Bat reached down and frisked him. The other was out cold.

Bat Hardin grunted satisfaction as he retrieved the Gyro-jet pistol which had been taken from him the previous morning. He stuck it into his belt and returned to his car.

He said into the car phone screen, "Okay, Al, back to full speed. Ignore the seeming corpse at the side of the road, if he's still there when you go by. He's just unconscious. Ran into my fist by accident."

"Fun and games," Al said.

Bat said to Luke, even as he got his car under way, "Everybody still keeping up?"

"Seem to be," Luke said.

They rolled on past the tiny town of Iturbide, also still asleep, only one or two sleepily shuffling locals on the streets, going about the duties of those whose work demands early rising.

Bat was doubly alert now and unconsciously chewing away at his lip. He said to Al and Luke, "That fellow I slugged knew that we were coming."

Luke said, "How could he have, Bat?"

"Somebody told him."

There was no answer to that.

They were getting out of the mountains now, and Bat Hardin felt moderately happier. He hadn't liked being caught in the canyons, mountain crags to both sides that could have sheltered snipers. For that matter, an enemy knowledgeable about dynamite could have, with a comparatively small charge, set off an avalanche that might have buried a score of homes. And he might have done it in such a manner that the police would have had their work cut out finding evidence that the landslide had not been an act of God.

However, they left the mountains behind them and shortly passed still another small hamlet, Puerto Pastores. By now, the morning was more advanced and a score of Mexicans stood watching New Woodstock go by. Evidently, mobile towns were more of a novelty on this by-road than they were on the larger highways.

It was only forty-five kilometers to San Roberto and Bat realized that they were going to make it to the Pan American Highway without difficulty. If there was going to be an attack, it would already have taken place. The best spots for an ambush were all behind them. Don Caesar's vigilantes simply hadn't materialized.

It had been a bluff. A well-acted bluff, but a bluff. However, Bat still didn't like it. Something didn't quite ring true. He had no doubt about the sincerity of Don Caesar, José and the others. They desperately wished to end the flood of mobile towns that were inundating their country. But what possibly could have been accomplished by the phony threat? Of course, a hundred homes had turned back but that wasn't a drop in the bucket. The vigilantes had accomplished nothing to end the flow of more than twenty towns and cities a day coming over the border.

He put it from his mind.

Shortly, they came to the end of Route E-60 and

entered the wide Pan American Highway at the town of San Roberto. Without halting, Bat Hardin turned left and headed south. He had, thus far, continued to remain a full two kilometers before the convoy but now he dropped speed until Al Castro caught up with him.

Bat said into the phone screen, "Okay, we can relax a bit now. However, still no stragglers. I want to put as much distance as possible between us and Linares."

"Righto," Al said, "The precautions didn't hurt us any." He yawned. "I didn't really expect anything to happen anyway. We have something like four hundred men with guns in this town. You'd need a small army to take us."

Bat flicked Al and Luke off his phone screen and dialed a road map of this vicinity and checked it. The Pan American Highway at this point wasn't automated so they'd have to remain on manual controls. That was all right with him.

He flicked the map off and said, "New Woodstock, Dean Armanruder."

Armanruder's face faded in. He was evidently sitting next to Nadine Paskov in his swank electro-steamer which drew one section of his mobile mansion. Bat knew that usually Manuel Chauvez drove the other section and that his wife, Concha, drove the smaller mobile home which was the living quarters of the two servants.

Dean Armanruder said testily, "See here, Hardin, the past hundred kilometers and more I've several times tried to get in touch with you to give instructions. I couldn't get you."

"Sorry, sir," Bat said. "I've had my screen on Al Castro and Luke Robertson continually so we'd be in instant touch if anything came up."

"Well, what did you call me for now?"

"I suggest we drive all the way through to San Luis Potosi and put as much space between us and our anti-American friends as we can. It's a fairly big city and listed as having several sites. You could call ahead, to be sure, for reservations for New Woodstock."

"How far is it?"

"Three hundred and twenty kilometers."

"That's a pretty long drag for a mobile town."

"Yes, sir, but we've got an early start. And I suggest we not stop for lunch."

The former magnate said testily, "Is this going to be a recommendation of yours every day, all the way to Peru?"

Bat said, "No, sir. I'm in no more of a hurry, ordinarily, than anyone else but the sooner we get a good many kilometers between us and Don Caesar and his boys the happier I'll be."

"It seems to me, Hardin, that you're taking over a good deal of the running of this town."

Bat sighed inwardly. "Not deliberately, Mr. Armanruder. But I'm the town cop and we were being threatened."

"Well, just remember that New Woodstock is governed by an executive committee elected by the citizens."

Bat said, but gently, "Whose decisions have to be passed upon by the assembly of all town adults."

"Of course. Very well, Hardin, I'll put it to the vote, whether to press on all the way to San Luis Potosi and to skip stopping for lunch." His face faded.

Bat grunted. He sometimes wondered at his desire to hold down this job. What did he get out of it? Not even a bit of gratitude from such as Dean Armanruder and the open dislike of such as Jeff Smith.

Bat Hardin wondered who had voted for that worthy

to take over Bat's office. But then it came to him. Whoever the traitor was that had kept Don Caesar and his people informed as to the movements of the town had also wanted Bat out and someone less competent in the crucial office of town police officer. That was an interesting thought.

San Luis Potosi was the most modern and progressive Mexican city they had as yet seen. Situated, as it was, on the Pan American Highway and the principal route from the States to Mexico City, it was well-equipped with sites for mobile towns. In fact, they spread out far over the countryside and, in area, were actually larger than the city itself, though it would seem doubtful if all the sites were ever completely occupied at one time.

There were three grades of sites, the smallest, ultraluxurious with a fine complement of stores, restaurants and even nightclubs and theatres. The least well-equipped was by far the largest and was aimed at mobile towns and cities largely occupied by persons with no other income than their NIT. However, even the accommodations at this site must have seemed exotic to the average Mexican, if the complaints of Don Caesar and his men were to be taken literally.

Dean Armanruder had called ahead for reservations and had been accepted, in spite of the fact that two other towns were at present parked in San Luis Potosi, evidently, like New Woodstock, on their way through to points further south. Their town, art colony that it was, seldom took on the expense of renting space in sites of the more swank variety. Although some of New Woodstock's citizens were wealthy, a considerably larger element were on NIT and had to watch expenditures. Here, in San Luis Potosi, they drove to the cheapest site available.

Bat Hardin, as usual, parked near the administration building and before setting up his own home drifted about the town to see that all was well. Evidently it was. They'd had excellent luck all day with not a single breakdown. The town had kept well together, much more so than usual. New Woodstock's artists were usually apt to be on the philosophical side and sometimes, on a long haul, the town might be stretched out several hundred kilometers. In fact, often single units or small groups would drop behind for days. It made life a misery for the town policeman who would have preferred more cohesion.

Bat, sauntering alone, passed Jeff Smith who was setting up his overly large home; overly large in view of its single occupant. Smith's mobile home wasn't nearly so big as that of Armanruder or Blake, nor even Sam Prager's, although the Prager establishment included the workshop, of course.

Jeff Smith looked up at him and snorted contempt. "Vigilantes," he said.

Bat ignored him and went on. He was afraid that the southerner wasn't going to make out in New Woodstock. Actually, he was sorry. He couldn't like the man, but Smith was the only musical composer that the art colony boasted and could have been expected to break down, eventually, and have presented some of his work at community affairs.

All seemed in order, but everyone so tired from the strain of the day and the long drive that it was a matter of a quick evening meal and then to bed. Bat returned to his own home and went through the automatic motions of setting it up.

He went inside and dialed himself a tequila sour on

the automatic bar. He could use the drink; he'd been through a lot, and had gotten precious little sleep the last couple of nights.

Glass in hand, he slumped into the most comfortable chair and automatically looked over at his small collection of books. But, the hell with it, he was too tired to read.

On his phone screen, he dialed the local road map again and checked. Queretaro was the next major city, two hundred and three kilometers to the south. That would probably be their next stop. It was far enough, in that they'd been pushing themselves for the past several days. They had made their decision to make the trek to South America while parked in the vicinity of New Orleans and had kept on the road since then. Some of the younger children, in particular, were getting tired. He supposed that they would make at least a several days' stop at Mexico City to rest up, make any repairs that had accumulated, shop for major items that might not be available in the smaller cities to the south, and allow time for those who had never seen the Mexican capital before doing some sightseeing. He checked. Oaxaca was a fairly good-sized town but otherwise the next major city to the south of Mexico City was Guatemala, in that country.

There was a knock on his door and he said, "Come on in."

It was Diana Sward, for once wearing a shirt, due to the cool of the Mexican evening.

She looked about the room and swore, "Damn it, every time I come into a bachelor's home I notice all over again how much neater you are than a single female. Why don't you mess it up a little, just in the way of creating an air of comfort?"

He laughed at that, even as she sank down onto the couch, without invitation, stretching her long shapely legs out before her.

He didn't ask her the reason for her visit. It wasn't the first time Di Sward had dropped in to chat. Alone, as was he, she sometimes spent a couple of hours with him just for the companionship. Diana Sward was a man's woman, and didn't particularly have any close feminine friends. There was something in her that the other women didn't seem to take to. Not that she had active foes in New Woodstock, to any extent, it was just that she wasn't the type to sit about and exchange gossip with the town's married women.

He went over to the bar. "Drink?"

"Do you have pseudo-whiskey?"

"No, you can't have whiskey."

"Why not?"

"Because you're in Mexico. Drink the local product. In Mexico, drink tequila, mescal or Kahlua."

"You're a hard man, Hardin. What's Kahlua?"

"A liqueur based on coffee," he told her. "And one of the best liqueurs in the world."

"Sounds too sweet. What are you drinking?"

"A tequila sour."

"You talked me into it."

He dialed another tequila sour and took it over to her and then returned to his own chair.

They sipped for a moment in silence. Finally, she said, "Remember that conversation we had about I.Q.?"

"Sure."

"I've been thinking about it. I wonder if the question has ever occurred to anyone, is it desirable to breed for greater intelligence?"

He scowled at her. "How do you mean, Di?"

125

"Well, take greater height. Why is being a six-footer or over desirable? Why is the average height of the Japanese, slightly over five feet, not just as good, or better? Certainly, in the old days when men slugged it out with swords, or when they worked with a shovel or plow, physical size was desired, but why now? We don't usually think of a man who weighs over two hundred as being in the best of shape, but we seem to have an absolute mania to be over six feet and to have a genius-level I.Q. Why? Has it ever been indicated, not to say proven, that the man with an I.Q. of 150 is happier than one with an I.Q. of 100? The genius, as well as the moron, is a misfit in society. Do we want to be smarter, or happier? If it is the pursuit of happiness that is our primary interest, then perhaps we should not seek, as a race, a high intelligence quotient."

Bat thought about it, for some reason slightly irritated. The subject was not a favorite one with him. He said, finally, slowly, "Man is a thinking animal, Di. If it wasn't for our superior intelligence we never would have gotten out of the caves."

"All right. I'm not contending that we ought to breed for morons, just that we also shouldn't make a fetish of the highest I.Q.s. Back when we were in the caves both intelligence and physical strength were necessary or the individual perished. So our I.Q. was bred up."

Bat said, "As a matter of fact, I understand that not only Cro-Magnon but even Neanderthal man had a larger brain than modern man."

"All right. But what I meant is, man has largely licked the problems he was confronted with in his infancy. We've defeated our animal enemies. We've conquered nature, at least to the extent that we can now produce all of our needs in abundance. All right. Isn't it time we took stock and decided where we want to go from here? We've achieved the necessities of life, now shouldn't we resume the pursuit of happiness?"

"Whatever that is," Bat said sourly. "Anyway, it's a great idea that possibly the average person, with his I.Q. of 100, is just as happy, or possibly happier, than one with 150. The trouble is, under the Meritocracy, I.Q. is what counts. And if you're ambitious and want to get ahead in present-day society, you'd best have one in the upper brackets."

She set her glass down and leaned forward slightly. "That's what I mean. Maybe Ferd Zogbaum is correct. Maybe this Meritocracy of ours isn't the end of the line so far as social evolution is concerned, if there's ever an end."

Bat said impatiently, "It's true that in production today not *all* jobs require a high intelligence. There are various operations, the sensory-manipulative operations that are involved in handling a power shovel, for instance, which have no appreciable educational or intellectual requirements and which do not lend themselves to automatic processes. But the overwhelming majority of useful jobs today do require high I.Q. and there is simply little place for we who are not particularly bright, to put it bluntly."

It was her turn to shake her head in despair. "You still sound like a goddamned professor of something or other to me," she said. "And here you say you're subnormal intellectually. But that was the very point I was trying to make."

He regarded her, still frowning.

She said urgently. "Don't you see? All members of society should be useful members of society. If they aren't, something snaps sooner or later. Look at the Roman proletariat. At present, under the Meritocracy, things are temporarily going along well enough, perhaps. The people were raised too long in the tradition that it was a good thing to get something for nothing, feather-bedding, and so forth. Beating the rap was admirable; they even idealized bankrobbers and other criminals. But now that the ultimate in pay without work has been reached, the first stirrings of second thought are to be found. I think that instinctively a man strives. He may be seduced away from the desire to work, to strive. He may, but if so it is a temporary thing, as the history of the race goes. Man wants to work and achieve. The so-called fireman sitting in the cab of a locomotive seven hours a day without a single thing to do, since the loco-motive is electric, is not a happy man. Certainly, the pay is good, and everybody tells him he is getting away with it, but he isn't a happy man. If he is, he's a sick man. If his fellows were contemptuous of him rather than pre-tending admiration, he'd get himself something else to do."

Bat made a gesture of impatience. "But the fact re-mains that there is no place for us in modern produc-tion. A fraction of the people can handle all of the jobs. Maybe it's not good for the rest of us to sit around, idle, but there's no alternative."

She leaned forward still further, her elbows on her knees and her voice very earnest.

She said, "Then we've got to make some changes. Back before we licked the problems of production of abundance that was, and had to be, the main goal of the race. Food, clothing, shelter, medicine, education, rec-reation for all, in abundance. But now that we've gained the goals, let's stop a minute and look around. How about the arts, how about the handicrafts? Ours has become a synthetic world, why not devote these sur-

128

plus energies of ours, devote the leisure time that hangs so heavily, into some of the old virtues? My grandfather mentions that when he was a boy practically everybody played some musical instrument. There was a bandstand in every park and at least one band in every town, no matter how small. Women used to sew, knit, crochet, embroider, make quilts and so forth. Have you ever seen some of those handmade quilts in a museum and compared them with the mass-produced things that we put on our beds today?"

Bat was chewing away on his lip. He said, "Some people already go into the arts; yourself, for instance. But not everybody has talent. And most are too lazy, if they don't have to, to bother with doing ceramics, weaving cloth, quilting, or whatever."

"Perhaps they are now, but that's our problem," she told him. "We've got to educate our people to want to do them. Take cooking. Cooking has become automated —and it tastes like it. Why, the person who could afford decent food a hundred years ago wouldn't have dreamed of eating the tasteless stuff that we down these days. Never has food been more beautifully packaged, been so adulterated, and tasted so poorly. And music. For all practical purposes, it's all canned these days. Sometimes I think that a few dozen musicians are turning out all the music for the country. How long has it been since you've seen a live musician? How long has it been since you've seen live theatre?"

Bat said doggedly, "It doesn't make sense in this day for there to be live theatres, employing tens of thousands of actors, when a cast of twenty can entertain fifty million persons at a time over TV."

"Like hell it doesn't," she said. "That's exactly the point I was trying to make. I'm beginning to suspect that

Ferd is right. Our present society needs a little subverting. What time is it?" She brought her pocket phone from her jeans and dialed for the time.

"Good Jesus," she said. "Is it that late? I better get going. I assume we're off to a fairly early start .in the morning."

Bat shrugged. "Not necessarily. We'll probably only go about two hundred kilometers, so there's no rush to get rolling." He stood to show her to the door.

But Diana didn't return immediately to her own trailer.

Her sexual binge with Ferd Zogbaum had been possibly the most satisfying she had ever known. It wasn't just that her lover had been tireless, though heavens knew he was possibly the only man she had ever slept with who had truly satiated her. It was also that they were in rapport. He obviously liked her, was attracted to her, as much as she was to him. It is difficult to prevaricate in bed, in a sexual relationship, or, at least, she had always thought so. She knew, instinctively, that he adored her body. She also knew, from the easygoing association she had had with the aspiring writer over the past weeks, that he was intellectually compatible with her.

Now she approached his camper and knocked at the door. She made no effort at all to be stealthy. Not in New Woodstock. Nobody could have cared less if she was having an affair with the popular Ferd Zogbaum. In fact, if anybody discovered the development they undoubtedly would have been happy for them both. Probably half of the so-called married folk in town were actually living in what was once known as sin.

She knocked at the door.

He opened and looked at her and made a humor-face and said, "Oh, no, not again."

"Oh yes," she said. "Stand aside, young man. We're going to play yes and no once more."

"I surrender."

She said, "Oh, darling, whatever is going to happen to us?"

"Yes."

"But it can never be a normal relationship. Not with you continually having to be on guard with everything you say to me."

"No."

"I love you, Ferd Zogbaum."

There was no answer. They kissed again, hotly.

"There is no answer, is there, darling?"

"No."

"Even if it was possible for us to have a . . . permanent relationship, they wouldn't allow it, would they? I'm an alien, an off-beat artist, a Bohemian—"

"Yes."

"You mean they wouldn't allow it?"

"Yes."

She slumped a bit in his arms. "All we can have is this?"

"Yes."

"Or they'll drag you back to prison—or to more brain surgery?"

"Yes."

"Let's get undressed."

They were resting between bouts.

She said, "Ferd, can you answer yes or no questions about this conspiracy to commit subversion against this government of yours?"

He hesitated for a long moment before saying cautiously, "Yes."

131

"They can't monitor your thoughts as such, eh? Just the words you think and if you get emotionally upset by committing violence."

He hesitated again.

She said, "There's more to it then that, eh?"

"Yes."

"Well, I don't suppose I'd understand it even if you could explain. Brain surgery isn't exactly my strong point. Did you belong to an organization in the States?"

Hesitation. Then, "Yes."

"Whose purpose was to start a new kind of government?"

"Yes."

"Was it a very large organization?"

"No."

"Do you think someday it will win out?"

Ferd hesitated still once again before saying, "Yes."

It was an extremely difficult manner in which to learn much about what he believed in. She knew perfectly well that he would have preferred to answer in more detail, to have qualified some of his yes and no answers.

She would have liked to find out just what this organization of Ferd's foresaw as a more desirable socio-economic system than Meritocracy. But it was too complicated a question under the circumstances.

Something came to her. "Could you write out answers to questions I asked you?"

"No."

"Hmmm. That's one hell of a complicated electronic bug they've planted in your bonnet, friend."

"Yes."

XV

Bat Hardin had been right. New Woodstock was slow to get underway the following morning. It was almost eleven o'clock before they began to roll.

Dean Armanruder was impatient with Bat but yielded to his demand that the mobile town remain in tight convoy again this day.

Bat led the way down the Pan American Highway, about a kilometer in advance of the town proper. Al Castro, driving today rather than his wife Pamela, was in Bat's usual place immediately ahead of the column. Luke Robertson brought up the rear. They were utilizing the same system as they had the day before. On the town phone system, Bat had once again emphasized the need for no one dropping out.

All went without incident for the first 120 kilometers, then ahead of him Bat spotted an official-looking car, two uniformed men next to it. There was a crossroads, and a barrier blocked the highway they were proceeding along. The sign on the barrier read *Desviasion* and an arrow pointed to the right.

Bat pulled up and one of the uniformed Mexicans came over and touched the peak of his hat in an informal salute.

Bat Hardin said, "What's up?" not knowing whether or not the other spoke English.

"Desviacion," the other told him in passable English.

"What you call a detour, Senor. The road is being worked upon a couple of kilometers ahead."

The Mexican brought forth a road map from his hip pocket and traced on it with a finger. "It is not much difference in distance. You go over here toward Dolores Hidalgo and then turn south to San Miguel de Allende. Then you come out at Queretaro, here." He shrugged. "Actually, Senor, it is a much more beautiful drive than this one, although, admittedly, the road is not so good."

Bat shrugged too. "Okay." he said. "A detour's a detour and there's nothing you can do about it."

The other turned and went back to his own car.

The mobile art colony was beginning to catch up with him. He raised Al Castro on his phone and said, "There's a slight detour. We turn right."

"Okay as she goes," Al yawned. "Sure is hotter than hell today. I hate heat." Al also hated cold, when it was cold and rain when it rained, as Bat Hardin recalled.

Bat flicked him off and proceeded.

He dialed the local road map and checked out the route of the detour. As the Mexican had said, it didn't lengthen their trip by very much. The road, as the other had told him, wasn't nearly as fine as the Pan American Highway, but it was adequate. There seemed to be no traffic whatsoever, which mildly surprised him. But then, of course, there weren't nearly the number of vehicles in Mexico as there were in the States and this was a by-way.

Before reaching the historic Dolores Hidalgo which, Bat vaguely recalled, was the town where the Mexican revolution against Spain in the early 19th century had begun, the road turned south. Before him he could see mountains rising but in this vicinity, although there were some hills and rises, largely the terrain was flat and covered with cactus and mesquite. Attractive enough, in sort of a wasteland way, but not exactly an area where one would build a home.

Suddenly his screen flicked on and Luke Robertson's face was there, his eyes were wide and wild. Bat!" he yelped. "I'm under fire and . . ."

The screen blanked and Luke's face was replaced with an abstract of meaningless flashing colors.

A barrage of screaming bullets ricocheted off the armor of Bat Hardin's converted police car. Across the fields, he could see large scurrying groups of men, rifles in hands, running and firing, converging on New Woodstock.

"Holy smokes," he blurted.

He banged the activating switch of his car TV phone and snapped into the screen, "Mexican Highway Police. Mexican Highway Police. Emergency. Emergency!"

The screen still ran impossible colors.

He slewed the car to the left, presenting the far side to the fire from the attackers. He grabbed his portable phone from his pocket, activated it and yelled, "Mexican Highway Police! Emergency. Emergency!"

But that screen too was a meaningless melange of streaks of moving color. Bat banged out the side of his car and crouching, darted back to Al Castro's vehicle, now immediately behind him. Al was driving, Pamela seated next to him, her pudding face a lard gray and her eyes in shock. Al was firing over her through her window with his Gyro-jet pistol, his face wild with excitement.

Bat shouted, "Al! Your car phone! Does it work?"

The magazine of his deputy's gun was evidently now empty. Al slammed the phone on. The color was there again, otherwise nothing at all.

135

Bat groaned, "They've got some sort of a scrambler on us. Al, out over the fields! Lead the town into a complete circle. Bumper to bumper. Take off."

"Got it," Al Castro yelped, starting up his electro-steamer again.

Bat hustled back to his own vehicle and fetched his carbine.

Al Castro took out over the cactus-strewn fields, bumping and bouncing, his mobile home careening every which way behind him.

Jake Benton, his eyes bugging, was immediately behind Al. Bat Hardin yelled to him from the shelter of the rear of his police car.

"Follow Castro! Form a circle! Form a circle! Then get out and return the fire!"

Benton's mobile home, careening as wildly as Al Castro's before him, took out over the desolate field.

Sam Prager's vehicles were next. Bat yelled, "Auxiliaries to the middle! Form a second circle. Hospital and school in the center!"

Sam nodded, gripped his wheel fiercely and was out after the others. Bat glared right and left. The attackers were largely on the minor hills and knolls and too far off for really accurate fire, although they were closing in fast. However, occasional slugs were still bouncing off the other side of his car. He winced to realize that none of the other vehicles in the town had any pretensions of being bulletproof.

The foe seemed to be in all directions and from Luke's warning, before the phones had gone out, were in the rear of the convoy as well. Perhaps Bat had made a mistake; perhaps he should have tried to bust on through. But no. Sure as green apples, they had some sort of roadblock up ahead.

He brought his carbine to his shoulder and snapped off a shot at one of the foremost of the attackers and had the satisfaction of seeing the man drop his gun and go flat forward on his face. It was the first man Bat had fired at since the war years.

"That'll make 'em a little less ardent," he muttered.

He continued to yell directions as the homes went by. Out in the field, Al Castro, avoiding mesquite trees but plowing right over all but the largest cactus plants, was making his circle.

Bat fished inside the car and located a fresh clip for his Gyro-jet carbine. He fired and fired again, in between directions for the arriving electro-steamers and mobile homes.

When the hospital, one section of which was being driven by Doc Barnes himself, came up, Bat yelled, "The hospital and school to the very center. Women and kids into them! They've got the thickest walls, for soundproofing. Older women and kids into school and hospital!"

Doc Barnes nodded grim acceptance of that and took off after the others, his section of the hospital bobbing desperately behind.

Al Castro's car and drawn home were beginning to come up from the rear on the tail end of the last of the New Woodstock column, but even after the circle had been drawn, with Luke Robertson's vehicles at the very end, Al continued to circle, slowing down, getting as near bumper-to-bumper as possible. He was obviously trying to tighten to the point where it would be difficult for the attackers to get through the spaces between vehicles.

Bat Hardin snapped off two or three more rounds, then jumped back into his car and took off after them. Luke Robertson slewed to one side, to let him through. Bat drove to the center and popped out. All the auxiliaries had been drawn, as directed, in a smaller circle; within were hospital and school which a dozen men were setting up as rapidly as possible in the mounting confusion.

Bat yelled at the top of his voice, the voice he had used in combat for those too many years in the Asian war, "All with guns take positions behind your homes. All without, get shovels. Dig foxholes; throw up dirt. All with more than one gun, turn them over to your neighbors without. All women with children, into hospital or school. Lie down on the floors. All women under forty, without children, get guns or shovels. If you have no shovels, frying pans. Dig in! This is the most important thing now, dig in!"

Children were screaming, women calling and crying. Half of the town was running about in a hash of confusion. There were a score of cases of hysteria. Doc Barnes, already in efficient action, was running around giving hypos to these.

Jeff Smith came up with what was evidently a high velocity varmint rifle with a telescopic sight under his arm. He was at least calmly collected.

He looked around at the preparations Bat had ordered and which were now fully underway and said, "I understand you were in the Asian war. What was your rank?"

Bat took him in. He said, wearily, "First lieutenant, when it ended. I was in for several years."

Jeff Smith cocked his head a little. "You don't look like the type that's been through OTS."

Bat said impatiently, "I was battle-commissioned during the Delta debacle."

Smith nodded. "I was at the Delta. 8th Airborne. Staff Sergeant. What are your orders . . . sir?"

Bat took a deep breath. "Move around the circle,

locating any other veterans we have. Spot them strategically. Be sure they all have the best weapons we have, even if you have to confiscate them from the others . . . Sergeant."

"Yes, sir." Jeff Smith turned and crouched, the crouch of the combat soldier in action, and hurried in the direction of the perimeter.

Luke Robertson and Al Castro came up at a trot.

"Wow!" Al shouted, over the blast of the shotguns, the snip of twenty-twos and other small-caliber gunfire, the snap of sporting and converted surplus military rifles.

Bat rapped, "Al, get around the circle. Cut down on this goddamned fire. We'll be out of ammo in half an hour. Cut the fire down to men with longer-range rifles and our best shots. Cut those goddamned shotguns out. They can't reach a fraction of the range these guys are at. The same with those damned twenty-twos. They can't dent a man unless you can get him in the head. Hold 'em down till they're close enough to hit 'em in the head."

"Right, Bat." Al scooted away. He too crouched the way Jeff Smith had crouched when he ran, almost double. Bat grunted inwardly. He hadn't known it. Evidently, Al Castro had seen a bit of combat himself in his time.

There was a whoosh of sound and beyond them a mesquite tree erupted in flame and explosion.

Bat closed his eyes in pain. "Holy smokes," he protested. "A bazooka."

Luke said, pointing excitedly, "It came from over there on that knoll, Bat."

Bat Hardin began gnawing his lip in agitation. "That's an old model, probably far back as the Second War. God only knows where they got it. But it's out of range. Listen, Luke, go around and locate our best riflemen. They'll know who they are. Get our best long-range rifles into their hands, those with telescopic sights. The hunting buffs have some of them. Pin that bazooka down. If they get within range, we're mincemeat."

Luke was off, scurrying low as he left the semi-security of the inner circle of auxiliary vehicles.

Bat Hardin cast his eyes around the complete circle of the horizon. They'd been jumped in an isolated spot indeed. Now he realized that the detour had been a plant. Don Caesar's men had directed them out here. He also realized why they hadn't been seeing other vehicles along this by-way. Somehow, the enemy had blocked it off. In all directions now they were surrounded. Single men and small groups were edging closer, darting in, scurrying around for cover. Closing in, closing in. But the fire had fallen off. Evidently, the anti-American vigilantes hadn't expected this efficient a defense.

Bat had been busy, hadn't been able to follow the combat incident by incident. He suspected that the Mexicans had taken a few casualties at the hands of the better shots, the war veterans and the amateur hunters among the art colony residents.

His lips thinned back. "Come in and get us, you bastards," he muttered.

Two men went by with an improvised stretcher. Doc Barnes came hurrying out of the hospital and bent over the victim.

Bat called, "Is he hit bad?"

Barnes looked up. "It's Thompson. He's dead."

Bat winced. Fred Thompson had the biggest family in New Woodstock. Five children.

Bat said to the stretcher bearers, "Bury him immediately. We don't want any of our dead lying around where they can be seen. Bad for the morale."

Little Chuck Benton came up excitedly. "Mr. Hardin, what should I do?"

Bat looked at him. The boy was eleven or twelve. He began to order him to the shelter of the s chool, then pulled up. He said, "Get a bucket of water and a dipper or cup, son. Go around to the men. Combat is dry work."

"Yes, sir." The youngster scurried off.

Bat looked after him. "Gunga Din," he muttered meaninglessly.

Crouching low, as Smith, Castro and Robertson before him, he left the shelter of the auxiliaries and scurried for the perimeter of mobile homes, his carbine in hand. He began touring it, barking orders for more rapid digging of foxholes.

Art Clarke came hurrying up to him, a more than usually large gun in hand. Bat Hardin recognized it. He snapped, "Isn't that a Chinese Am-8? Where in the hell did you get it?"

Even in this excitement, Clarke seemed slightly embarrassed. He said, "War souvenir."

"Fully automatic? How many clips do you have for it?"

"Yeah. It's the Canton model. Two clips."

"How much spare ammo?"

"I've got possibly two hundred rounds."

Bat looked quickly around, spotted the man he could use and yelled, "Milt Waterman! Over here."

The tall, gangling young fellow who usually drove the administration building when New Woodstock was rolling, came hustling up.

Bat rapped, "You two, get into that hole over there. Get that automatic rifle set up. Milt, you keep the spare clip loaded. Art, you let loose a burst of fire from time to time. A longer burst than you'd expect from a gun that light. I want to make it look as though we've got a machine gun. Wait a minute. After you've let loose a couple of bursts from this side, go to the direct opposite and do the same. Make it look as though we've got *two* machine guns. Keep moving back and forth. But go easy. Stretch out that ammo as much as you can. Don't fire unless you've got a fairly good chance of winging your man."

"Got it," Art Clarke said and took off to follow orders.

Bat went on.

Diana Sward was sitting on the ground at the rear of her mobile studio. She had a sporting rifle in her hands and her elbows were on her knees as she periodically and with great coolness squeezed off a shot.

"Watch the ammunition," Bat told her, beginning to go by.

She grinned up at him, her eyes shining. "I think I nicked at least one. You know what this reminds me of? A wagon train, surrounded by Sitting Bull's braves."

"It is," he said grimly and hurried on. He heard a bee buzz past his head. That had been a close one.

He came to Dean Armanruder's mobile mansion. Armanruder, his back tight against the side of one of the sections, his face pasty, screamed at him.

"Do something!"

Bat looked at him quizzically. "What? We're doing all we can. They've got a scrambler out there somewhere. We can't call for help."

"Surrender! Tell them we'll do anything! We've got money. Anything they want!" The older man was panting, the stink of fear on him. "Tell them we'll do anything they say."

Bat Hardin shook his head as though in an attempt to

142

clear it. Two more of the men without guns went by, carrying one of the hospital stretchers, an inert form on it.

Jeff Smith was approaching from the opposite direction to the one in which Bat had been circling the perimeter.

Bat said, "Sergeant, you and Al Castro. Improvise a white flag." He added sardonically, "My compliments to Don Caesar and ask him for his terms."

"Yes, sir." Crouching, Jeff Smith headed for the inner circle of auxiliaries.

Bat moved on. He passed Ferd Zogbaum who was digging coolly and efficiently a small trench. He had an army surplus entrenching tool. There were quite a few of the efficient compact tools in town, Bat knew.

Bat Hardin paused. The other didn't look up from his work.

Bat said, "Ferd, there's a scrambler on us. All electronic communication devices are disrupted."

Ferd looked up, his face registering surprise.

Bat said, before going on, "I doubt if that bug of yours is operative."

Jeff Smith and Al Castro came hurrying up. Smith had a white pillowcase tacked onto a broom handle with thumbtacks.

The Southerner said, "Any special instructions, Lieutenant?"

Bat shook his head. "Play it by ear. Tell them we'll go back. Tell them we pledge not to take any action against them, to the extent we can. Obviously, the Mexican authorities are going to get after them, in view of the casualties both sides have already taken. But so far as we can, we'll avoid prosecuting. Promise anything. Armanruder offered money, but he's hysterical. Those men out there aren't bandits."

"Yes, sir," Jeff said. "Come on, Castro."

The two leaned their guns against a mobile home and stepped out into the open, the improvised white flag held high. For a moment they stood there—obviously awaiting the impact of slugs before those out beyond could distinguish that they were seeking a conference.

Bat Hardin, his hands cupped to his mouth, was yelling, "Hold fire, hold fire, everybody!"

The firing of the defenders fell off. So did that of the attacking force. At least the flag of truce was being recognized. Bat hadn't been sure it would.

Smith and Castro began to walk forward. Shortly, down from one of the nearer knolls came two others. Even at this distance, the hair of one was obviously gray.

"Don Caesar," Bat muttered. He turned and called to Ferd, "Make the rounds. Get Tom Benton and a couple of the other men to go with you. Round up all the ammo we have, not already loaded into the guns. Take it into the enclosure of the auxiliaries and inventory it. Separate it into piles by caliber and gauge. Also inventory every gun we have, rifle, pistol, shotgun, by caliber and gauge. We've got to take rigid steps to conserve our munitions. We'll dole it out slowly."

Dean Armanruder came up, still quaking, his eyes glaring. He said shrilly, "What do you mean? What do you mean? We're surrendering. We'll do anything they say. I've got money. We can buy them off."

Bat ran his eyes over him and said finally, slowly, "Mr. Armanruder, those men out there think they're fighting for their country, their culture, their women and even their religion. It parlays up to quite a motive for fighting. On top of that, it hasn't been easy for them to organize this and put it over. They're not going to have a second chance, and they know it. The Mexican authorities are going to land on them like a ton of bricks. They'll have to or Uncle Sam will take measures. So they've got to put this over this time. Their strategy is obvious. They're going to make an example of us so frightful that no American mobile home would dream of coming to Mexico, and those already here are going to make a beeline for the border and never return."

"You're insane!"

"I hope so," Bat growled.

Several score of the men, guns in hand, had gathered around to watch after Smith and Castro who had by now met the delegation from the other side.

Bat said to them, "We've got one thing in our favor. They've got to finish us quickly. Somehow they've blocked the road both in front and behind but they can't keep that up indefinitely. A police patrol or someone else will stumble on what's happening. If we can stick it out until morning, we'll have it made."

Art Clarke said, "Great, but when night comes they're going to bring that bazooka into range, and then we've had it."

Bat said, half angrily, "That'll be all, Clarke. Don't put the damper on morale. They probably only have a few rounds for it. The thing's an antique. It's unlikely they could have rounded up more than few charges."

"We hope," Luke Robertson muttered.

Jeff Smith and Al Castro were on their way back. All stood in silence, waiting. More of those who had been in the foxholes came crowding up.

The two reentered the perimeter of mobile homes. Both of their faces were strained.

Bat said, "Well?"

Jeff Smith looked him in the face. He took a deep breath and said, "They'll grant no terms. They wouldn't even allow the women and children to come out under a truce flag. The old one said it was less brutal, in the long run, to make this example so crushing a one that it would be done once and for all." Smith snorted his disgust. "He sent his apologies, but said there was no alternative."

XVI

"So," Bat said. "A massacre." He turned to the assembled men. "Return to your positions. So long as they're still at this distance, restrain your fire. Only veterans and highly experienced marksmen with long-range rifles are to fire at all. Hold your small arms and shotguns until they're at point-blank range, which possibly won't come until nightfall."

Dean Armanruder shrilled, "No. No, don't listen to him! Don't shoot back at them! We'll all surrender. We'll go out with our hands up, in a body. They'll accept our surrender!"

"Like hell they will," Bat said in disgust. "Get back to your positions, men."

"Shut up, Hardin!" the former magnate yelled at him. "You're removed from your position as town police officer. I'm in command here!" He began going from group to group, yelling at the men, some of whom looked sheepish now.

Somebody grumbled, "Maybe he's right. If we all went out with our hands up . . ."

Jeff Smith looked at Bat Hardin.

Bat said, "Sergeant, put him under arrest and take him into the inner circle. Post a guard over him, one of the older men we can spare from the firing line. If he attempts further to destroy morale, shoot him."

Smith said, "Yes, sir." He turned and grabbed Ar-

147

manruder by the arm and hustled him away, jerking at the restraint and protesting hysterically.

The vigilantes were firing again, beginning to edge in again, dashing from one clump of cactus, or other cover, to the next. The circle about the mobile town was slowly narrowing.

Bat began making the rounds again, encouraging the marksmen, continually urging the conservation of ammunition. "You'll get your chance soon enough," he snapped to those with short-range weapons.

He came to Ferd Zogbaum who was seated nonchalantly in a foxhole, looking out over the field. He held a double-barreled shotgun in his hands but wasn't firing it.

Bat said, "See you got yourself a gun." He began to go on, to resume his constant patrol.

But Ferd looked at him strangely and said, "Bat, I've got a funny feeling."

Bat Hardin stopped and squinted at him.

"How do you mean?"

Ferd looked out over the field again and said, choosing his words carefully, "I have a premonition that that scrambler, or whatever you called it, is awfully nearby. Well, say within a couple of hundred yards or so."

"How do you know?"

"I don't. I just have that feeling."

Bat went on again, crouching, going from one foxhole to the next.

He came to Sam Prager who was crouched in a comfortably deep one-man entrenchment. Bat hunkered down on his heels and said, "Sam, tell me something about scramblers."

"Not much to tell," Sam said. "You wouldn't understand the workings unless you had some background in electronics."

"I haven't. How wide a range does one have?"

Sam scowled. "According to what kind you have. The military have some real doozies, blanket a wide, wide area."

"But would our pals out there be apt to have anything like that?"

Sam looked up into the sky, scowling still. "Well, no, now that you mention it. And they don't even have a helicopter."

"Why would they need a helicopter?"

"It'd give them more range. As it is, they've probably got it mounted on some high spot out there."

Bat took a deep breath. "Aren't they portable? Can't they be moving it around?"

"I wouldn't think so. They're pretty delicate mechanisms, Bat. They'd have to get it all set up. If they had to move it, it would be off for the time of moving and until they got it rigged up again."

Bat Hardin hissed between his teeth. Then, "Do I understand you that's it's got to be within sight of the area that it is blanketing?"

"Well, more or less. Part of it has to be. The antenna."

"So out there, somewhere, within sight, is our scrambler?"

"It's got to be."

Bat got up. The firing was growing slowly more intense from the other side, falling off on the part of the defenders who were becoming increasingly conscious of their depleted store of ammunition. New Woodstock had not been proceeding with any idea at all of a need for large stocks of cartridges and shells. Some weapons

149

had only a score or so rounds available which was the reason that Bat had pooled their supply. It was now being doled out grudgingly to the best shots.

Bat Hardin, again bent almost double as he scurried across the open space between the outer ring of vehicles and the inner, sought out Jeff Smith, who was busy supervising the digging of the trench that was to be their last stand, if it came to that.

Bat said, "Sergeant."

The Southerner came over and looked at him questioningly.

Bat pointed with his finger, swept it around the horizon. He said, "According to Sam Prager, the scrambler is somewhere out there in an elevated position. Probably on one of those knolls. We could make a sortie and destroy it."

"Yeah," the other said disgustedly. "But which knoll?"

Bat called over to Luke Robertson, "Luke, locate us a couple of pair of the strongest binoculars in town." Then he turned back to Jeff Smith.

"It seems that it takes a bit of time to set a scrambler up. Very delicate. And if you want to keep it in action, you can't move it. It's got to just sit there._Now our friend, Don Caesar, is no fool. He's figured out this raid to the last detail. He knows that our only chance is to get that scrambler and wreck it. He also knows that we have some four hundred armed and desperate men on hand for a sortie. So what does he do?"

Smith's forehead was wrinkled. "I'm not following you, Lieutenant."

"If one of those knolls out there was more strongly defended than any other, what would you suspect?"

"That's where the scrambler was."

"And if one knoll had no men around it all . . ."

Smith got it. "You mean the old bastard is trying to fox us by having that damn thing stuck up somewhere with nobody at all in the vicinity?"

"It's worth thinking about."

Luke came up with the glasses and handed them to Smith and Bat. They began to scan the vicinity slowly, carefully.

Bat murmured, "It would probably be one of the higher knolls, and one not too very far away. They planned this down to the last detail. They maneuvered us out into this field, as though we were sheep. They knew exactly where we'd have to go. And that scrambler was all set up and waiting for us when we arrived."

Jeff Smith said, "There it is, Lieutenant." He pointed. "I can just barely make out an antenna, or whatever it is."

Bat Hardin directed his glasses. "You're right. "Okay, Sergeant. It's you and me."

Smith looked at him. "Just the two of us? Wouldn't it make more sense if we took a hundred of the best men and headed for that knoll on the double?"

Bat shook his head. "My converted police car is the only armored vehicle in town and it's a two-seater. We have, in short, the equivalent of a tank. Can you operate an Am-8?"

"The Chinese automatic? Sure, why not?"

"Get Art Clarke's from him and both clips of ammo. I'll meet you at my car."

Jeff Smith took off and Bat Hardin called to Al Castro, "Al, let me have your Gyro-jet pistol."

Al handed it over. Bat Hardin checked the magazine, jacked a 9mm rocket cartridge into the barrel. He stuck the gun in his belt, then brought forth his own identical weapon and checked and loaded it. Then he went over to his car, located spare 9mm rocket shells and dropped them into his side pocket. He took up his carbine and filled the magazine to capacity.

"Jesus," Al said. "You look like Billy the Kid with all that artillery."

Bat said, "Al, get together our best half dozen marksmen. That knoll out there looks as though nobody at all is around. There's nobody firing from the top or anything. However, I'll bet my left arm that they've got a sizable defending force behind it, keeping hidden. Jeff and I are going to need all the covering fire we can get."

"Got you," Al said, moving off.

A dozen of the men who had been digging now stood around, popeyed at what Bat was planning.

Manuel Chauvez, shovel in hand, said, "Mr. Hardin, for sure, you are not going out there into all that fire?"

"Somebody's got to go, or we'll unlikely see tomorrow," Bat growled to the Armanruder's servant. "Come on, Sergeant. The delta was never like this."

"Thank the good Lord," Jeff Smith muttered. "It was bad enough." He had Art Clarke's automatic rifle under his arm and was stuffing the spare magazine into a side pocket. He climbed into the seat next to Bat's driver position.

Smith looked out over the terrain unhappily and said, "You think you can make it over that? You'd need at least a four-wheel drive."

Bat grinned. "I've got secrets in this buggy." He dropped the conversion lever, activated the air cushion and the vehicle rose a foot off the ground. He recessed the wheels and yelled out the window, "Luke, get that crate of yours out of the way."

"I'll be damned; a little old hover-car," Smith said.

Bat nodded while Luke hurried to get his electro-

152

steamer and mobile home out of the way so that the two volunteers could leave the perimeter.

Bat was saying, "They've got a lot of shortcomings but for certain specialized uses you can't beat the air cushion. Ordinarily they aren't practical for a vehicle of this size. Too small. Consume power like crazy. Can't propel them very fast, either, or your vehicle will over-run your air cushion. It's got to have time to get out in front of the skirt, or the whole shebang starts nosing in."

Luke yelled, "Okay, Bat!"

The police car, now air-cushion borne, flowed ahead.

Immediately, slugs began to bounce off in screaming ricochet.

"Holy smokes," Bat bit out. "You'd think they were waiting for us. Keep your window up until we get on the scene. Bulletproof glass. They'd have to have anti-tank shells to knock us off."

Smith said, "They don't need anti-tank shells, they've got that goddamned bazooka."

"Ummm," Bat said distastefully, beginning to zig and zag in evasive action. "But I've got a sneaking suspicion that the boys operating it aren't exactly crackshots. Who in the hell knows how to fire a bazooka in this day and age? It's one thing sitting pat and directing it at something as big as New Woodstock. But a target this small and on the move?"

"I hope you're right, Lieutenant," the other said dryly.

The knoll was perhaps three hundred meters away. Al's marksmen were going to have to be on their merit to do much in the way of covering. However, any fire at all was better than none, just so it didn't hit Bat or Jeff Smith.

Bat kept the car at as high a speed as was consistent

with the terrain and their air cushions, but they were doing fifty kilometers an hour at best. Occasional bullets continued to rain off their armor but thus far there had been no stirring of opponents on the knoll which was their destination. Bat began to wonder if they had guessed wrong. But no, it was more than a guess, the closer they got the more obvious was the antenna, stretching its evil feelers up into the sky, robbing them of contact with the outside world.

As they got nearer it became obvious that the car would never make it up to the summit.

Bat groaned, "These things are impossible on non-horizontal surfaces. They slip off in every direction except the one you want to go."

Jeff Smith bit out, "Get as far up as you can and then cover me. I'll make a run for it."

"Why not me?"

Smith said, "Because you know how to drive this contraption and I don't."

"All right."

Just as they hit the bottom of the slope, a half dozen Mexicans materialized at the summit and began firing down at them in great excitement.

Smith muttered, "Amateurs!" and activated the window. He steadied the Chinese automatic rifle on the sill and let loose a sweeping burst. Several went down, screaming pain, the others ducked for cover.

Jeff Smith was out of the car, gun in hand and zig-zagging up to the crest.

"Go it!" Bat yelled. He popped from the side of the car, both Gyro-jet pistols in his hands.

Jeff Smith scrambled, slid, fell, was on his feet again. Up he went.

At the top, one of the Mexicans who had fallen got

to his knees. He was holding some sort of automatic weapon with which Bat Hardin was unfamiliar. It stuttered and Jeff Smith fell off to the side and to the ground.

Bat fired twice and brought the gunner down. He started up the hill after his companion. From the perimeter of the mobile homes came a hail of supporting fire, sweeping the top of the small mesa.

Bat Hardin went to the smaller man. He jammed his pistols into his belt, swearing uncontrollably. "Bad?" he snapped, reaching down.

Jeff Smith groaned, "Yeah. Nailed me at least twice. Belly."

"Oh, Christ," Bat groaned. He hiked the other up over his shoulder, reached down and swept up the automatic and started staggering and stumbling down the hill.

A blow struck him in the right hip and he all but fell.

"Hit?" Jeff Smith groaned.

"Yeah."

He continued on, stumbling. He could feel the blood running down his leg.

They got to the car, on Smith's side. Bat dumped him in, tossed the Chinese weapon in after him, then hurried around the car, limping, dragging his leg, to his own side. He lifted his right leg by grabbing hold of the cloth of his pants and swung it into the cab. He wedged himself in, pulled Smith to a position so that he could close the door on that side. He swerved the car and headed back. He would have liked to make his own try for the crest but he doubted that his leg would allow him and, besides, Jeff Smith had to be gotten back to Doc Smith soonest. The Southerner was bleeding like a stuck pig.

Bullets were again caroming off the surface of the

vehicle. They retraced their route. Twice, Bat Hardin recognized the whoosh and trail of bazooka rockets but he had been right, they were far off the mark. Whoever was on the old-time rocket launcher was no marksman.

Luke Robertson's vehicles were still drawn out of the way and Bat Hardin maneuvered through.

He yelled out the window, "Jeff's been hit. Where's Doc Barnes?"

Barnes came hurrying forward, physician's bag in hand.

Jeff Smith, his face drained as death, looked over at his companion.

"Hey, man."

"Yeah?"

"Sorry about that nigger thing . . . Bat."

Bat shook his head. "Nothing to it . . . Jeff."

Doc Barnes wrenched open the door of the car and bent over Smith.

He looked up at Bat. "He's dead."

Bat Hardin didn't say anything for a moment. Two men were hauling Jeff Smith from the car, ridiculously gently in view of the fact that pain would never come to the small feisty Southerner again.

Bat said, "I've copped one too, Doc. See if you can patch me up a little."

"We'll get you out of the car and up to the hospital where I can do a better job."

Bat shook his head. "Can't. If I do, I'll never be able to get back in, and I'm the only one who can drive this thing. It takes a certain know-how." He looked at Luke. "Somebody in here tipped them that we were coming in this vehicle. Find Nadine Paskov. Have her check in the computer banks and find out who voted against me in that hassle I had with Jeff." He added sourly, "She's probably under some bed, somewhere. A change for her. I suspect that whoever cast that vote against me is our traitor. If she refuses to tell you, for whatever reason, slap her around a little."

"Got it," Luke said. "What'll I do if I find the traitor?"

Bat looked at him levelly.

"Got it," Luke said, and was off.

"Hold still, damn it," Doc Barnes said. "Let me get this bandage on you. You need plasma; you dripped too much ink, Bat."

"Oh, great," Bat said. "Have you got some kind of pep pill instead?" He looked out over the crowd and called, "Ferd, you're next."

"Coming up," Ferd Zogbaum sang out, pushing his way through the assembled men. He caught up the automatic rifle that had fallen to the ground when the men had taken Smith's body out, and scrambled into the bloody seat next to Bat.

Bat called, feeling himself already weaker, "There's an extra clip of ammo in Jeff's pocket."

Somebody brought it.

Bat Hardin activated the lift lever again and they started forward.

He explained as they went. "I can't get the car to the crest. You'll have to make it on foot. All hell is breaking loose over there. Don Caesar is sending new men over as fast as they can make it to defend the point. They know damn well, now, that we know it's there, and they've got to defend it." He felt his voice going weaker.

Next to him, Ferd Zogbaum was checking the clip

in the gun. Jeff Smith had nearly emptied it. Ferd threw it and rammed home the spare full clip with the heel of his hand.

Bat said weakly, "Where did you get checked out on the Chinese Am-8?"

Ferd said, "I was in the big one too."

They were approaching the knoll. From behind, the full barrage of all that New Woodstock could mount in the way of long-range rifles was firing over them, attempting to pin down any of the enemy forces on hand.

Bat ground to a halt. He pulled his two pistols out.

"Okay, Ferd. It's all yours."

Ferd was out of the car, automatic in hands and scurrying up the hill, slipping, sliding on the sandy terrain, going three feet up, sliding back at least one. A continual fire kicked up the dust around his feet but he miraculously remained erect. Bat, his eyes fogging, leaned out the window of the car and blasted away at anything that moved—save Ferd.

The freelance writer achieved the top, fired twice, thrice, in this direction and that, on full automatic, and finally immediately down as though toward his feet. He turned and began retracing his steps, running dangerously. He fell, rolled a score of feet, staggered erect, came on again.

"Come on boy, come on!" Bat pleaded.

Suddenly, Ferd Zogbaum stopped dead in his tracks. The automatic rifle dropped from his hands. He grabbed his head desperately and began to waver.

"The bug!"

He staggered around, completely out of control of himself, moaning in agony. A burst of automatic fire hit him.

Bat, reeling weakly himself, flicked on his phone and

stuttered, "Emergency, emergency! Mexican Police. Road Dolores Hidalgo, San Miguel de Allende. Emergency emergency, emer . . ." And then the fog rolled in.

When Bat Hardin became conscious again, he was in the mobile clinic of Doc Barnes. He felt weak, but his mind was alert. He looked about him. Ferd Zogbaum, unconscious, was in the next bed. It was a three-bed dormitory. The other bed was empty.

Doc Barnes came in followed by Diana Sward who was wearing a nurse's white smock. She was obviously a volunteer.

Barnes said, "You're awake. Good." He turned and looked down at Ferd Zogbaum.

Bat said, "How's Ferd?'

"He'll be all right. He took three hits, but none of them too serious. We're taking him in for some minor surgery now."

Bat said, "Listen, has he been unconscious all this time?"

Doc Barnes looked at him impatiently over his shoulder. "Why, yes."

Bat said, "Look, Doc. When you were in private practice what was your specialty?"

"Why, I was a surgeon."

"Brain surgeon?"

"No. I have done some brain surgery, but it was not my specialty."

Bat took a deep breath. "Look, Doc. Ferd Zogbaum is going to die on your operating table."

Di Sward blurted, "Don't be an ass."

He ignored her. "Doc, Ferd has an electronic device planted in his skull. Can you take it out?"

Barnes goggled at him.

Bat pursued. "He's a paroled convict. Life sentence. He saved us all. Look, Doc. We took a lot of casualties in this fracas. All is confusion. He can die on your operating table. You can sign . . . whatever it is you doctors sign when a guy cashes in his chips."

"I'm an ethical——"

"And you and everybody else in New Woodstock owe your life to Ferd Zogbaum."

Doctor Barnes held a long silence. Finally he said, "What was he sentenced to life for? I have heard of this electronic bug before but it is the first in my experience. It should not be difficult to remove. Is he a murderer?"

It was Di Sward who said heatedly, "He's an idealist! He has political objections to the present socio-economic system in the States."

Doc Barnes looked at her wryly. "You seem a bit partisan, Miss Sward. However, so do I. I don't exactly know what they are, but I too have reservations about our present socio-economic system. You are sure that Zogbaum's, ah, crimes, are all of a political nature?"

"Yes," Diana said firmly.

"Very well. Now the question becomes, if he, ah, dies on my operating table, and I remove the electronic device from his skull, how does he continue to collect his NIT or otherwise support himself?"

Bat and Diana looked at each other blankly.

Diana Sward said finally, "I make a reasonable living with my painting. He can write under a pseudonym until he gets to the point where he is making better sales. We'll never return to the States."

Doc Barnes took her in. "You are his mistress?"

She said, her mouth tight, "Yes, I am his mistress, and I am willing to become his wife—if he will have me. I am not a great acquisition."

"Like hell you aren't," Barnes said sourly.

Doc thought about it, his face in disgust. "Damn it," he said. "Why can't a doctor just carve them up, or slip them the necessary shots or pills?" He glared at Di. "Miss Sward, let's make the arrangements to get this operation rolling, before we have no patient left . . . to die on our operating table." He turned and left the room.

Diana Sward looked at Bat and said, "I think we've swung him. See you later, Bat."

"Yeah, see you later, Di," he said, looking after the woman he loved as she left the room.

Aftermath

The *Secretária de Defensa Nacional* colonel said courteously, "Your arrest was a technicality, of course. You are free to go at any time you wish, Senor Hardin. But, after all, several of our nationals were killed, including Caesar Munoz and his son, José."

"And several of our own citizens, Colonel," Bat Hardin said softly.

"Yes, including one that you killed yourselves, this Manuel Chauvez."

"He was caught signaling Don Caesar's son," Bat said. "He tried to resist arrest and Mr. Robertson was forced to shoot him. Evidently, he had what amounted to a mania against his employer and against Americans in general."

The colonel gestured to the TV screen on his desk. "As I said, your arrest was a technicality; however, to double check on you I secured your dossier from your American National Data Banks. Purely routine. Your record, I am pleased to see, is impeccable."

Bat said, "I should congratulate you people on the speed with which you came to our assistance. I was unconscious at the time but I understand that the helicopters were there in less than fifteen minutes."

The colonel nodded. "You see, we were aware of

162

Caesar Munoz's activities and his group was under observation. We knew they had desperate plans but weren't exactly sure what they were. Nevertheless, we had a sizable force on continual alert. Frankly, we were astonished at the magnitude of the attempt. Thank God he has failed."

Bat said unhappily, while gnawing at his lip, "Are you so sure that he has? What will happen when this affair hits the newspaper headlines?"

"It will not hit the headlines, Senor Hardin. The Mexican and United States governments are cooperating to suppress the account. We are aware of the problems brought on by the mobile towns, but Don Caesar's solution was not the correct one. He was trying to turn the wheels of time backward. It can't be done. Yesterday will never be with us again, whether we wish it to be or not."

"What is the solution?"

The colonel shrugged in a Latin gesture. "Perhaps I do not know. Perhaps it is more rapid progress for Mexico so that we, in turn, became an affluent society." He laughed abruptly. "You would be surprised, Senor Hardin, how rapidly the spread of mobile homes is coming to *our* country. We already have several mobile resort towns, some of which cross periodically to the United States. And, to the south, Guatemala has recently complained of the large number of Mexican homes and trailers that are flooding that country."

Bat came to his feet. "I should be going. New Woodstock is scheduled to head south today. All repairs have been completed. We must thank the Mexican government again, for taking on all expenses involved."

"Certainly it was the only possible thing for us to do,"

the colonel said, coming to his feet and extending his hand to be shaken.

He said, "Would you mind answering one question, Senor Hardin?"

Bat looked at him quizzically.

The colonel said, "I went over the details of the whole unfortunate affair. I must say, I admired your measures. I am sure Don Caesar never expected such a valiant defense."

"Thanks," Bat said.

"As a police officer myself, I find I am somewhat surprised that your talents are hidden away in such a small town as New Woodstock. Your war record is impressive." He gestured at Bat's dossier still in the screen on his desk phone. "Have you never considered attending one of your American police schools and then securing a position in one of your larger cities?"

Bat said evenly, "I'm not eligible."

The colonel frowned puzzlement. "But why?"

"My I.Q. is not adequate."

"Not adequate! We do not use the same system here in Mexico but I was under the impression that an I.Q. of 132 was quite superior."

"My I.Q. is 93, Colonel."

Frowning still, the colonel looked down at the dossier. "It says here, 132. You seem to have made some sort of a mistake, Senor Hardin."

Bat Hardin stood silently for a long moment. Then, without asking permission, he rounded the colonel's desk and stared down at the dossier in the screen.

Finally, he said softly, "Al Castro can take over my job."

The colonel's eyebrows went up. "You are not continuing with the rest of your town to the south?"

"No. I'm returning to the States to find my level. Perhaps Ferd Zogbaum was correct and there are basic changes to be made in the Meritocracy, but, if so, they'll be made from the inside, not from without."

"I wish you luck, Senor Hardin," the colonel said.